Award-winning autho
adventures of the hea
stories about alpha m
Australia for Mills &
her family in the San

If you liked *Best Laid Plans*, why not try

Make Me Crave by Katee Robert
Wild Thing by Nicola Marsh
Destroyed by Jackie Ashenden

Discover more at millsandboon.co.uk

K

BEST LAID PLANS

REBECCA HUNTER

MILLS & BOON

First Published in Great Britain 2018
by Mills & Boon, an imprint of HarperCollins*Publishers*
1 London Bridge Street, London, SE1 9GF

© 2018 Rebecca Hunter

ISBN: 978-0-263-93227-0

MIX
Paper from
responsible sources
FSC **FSC™ C007454**
www.fsc.org

This book is produced from independently certified FSC™ paper
to ensure responsible forest management.
For more information visit www.harpercollins.co.uk/green.

Printed and bound in Spain
by CPI, Barcelona

To my sister Leah, who tolerates early drafts of everything I write.

Your adventures in Australia inspired this series.

CHAPTER ONE

"LESS LIKE A fraternity and more like a real company? What the hell does that mean?"

Cameron Blackmore leaned back in the plush lounge chair and massaged his temples. He didn't like this any more than the others, but as CEO of Blackmore Inc. in Australia, he had to be the voice of reason. Or at least survival. He crossed his arms and looked each of the other three members of his team in the eye.

"You all know exactly what this means," he said. "After the recent news coverage we've gotten, we need to lie low for a while. We're in high-profile security, for fuck's sake. No public appearances, no partying and no walking out of a pub with clients."

Derek and Simon nodded. Max's scowl grew.

"Can your father and his board tell us where we can go and who we can bring home with us?" Max grumbled. "All the way from New York?"

Cameron surveyed the dark room and caught a couple glances in their direction from other patrons. Damn. They were attracting attention. He had moved their impromptu meeting to the hotel lounge to be discreet, but discreet wasn't Max's strong suit.

Cameron lowered his voice and leaned in. "It's not like any of us were planning on finding the love of our lives in the next two weeks." He turned to Max. "And to answer your question, yes. When you land on the front page of the *Sydney Morning Herald*, yes."

Derek and Simon looked at Max.

Max threw his hands up. "Hey, I was fact-finding with her."

Derek smirked. "Is that what you call it, mate?"

"We don't need to get into this again," said Cameron. "You did what you needed to do. The client understood that, even if the board doesn't. They're owned by my father, so what do you expect?"

His smile disappeared. Harlan Blackmore still managed to wield some control over his life, even a continent away. Cameron's dislike of his father was no secret. When he joined the family business, Cameron had expected his grandfather to hold on for a few more years. Enough time to take the ruins of the business his father had left in Australia and turn it into the kind of company his grandfather had built. Cameron had fond, if hazy, memories of Sydney from the two years he'd spent here as a child—back when his parents were together. So, he'd jumped on the opportunity to return a couple years ago. But his grandfather's heart attack wasn't in Cameron's plans, nor was his father's scramble for control over Blackmore Inc.

And Harlan Blackmore had no fucking idea how to

run an international security company. He just looked the part and acted the part, all while running Blackmore Inc. Australia into the ground with his US strategies. And the board rewarded him for this grand performance by making him president.

But maybe, just maybe, this whole recent turn of events could be Cameron's chance to run the business his way. His grandfather's way. A chance to show the board that focusing on a strong, loyal team and the demands of the current market had a better business payoff than making strategic golf partners or any of the other shit the board wanted him to do. His father could play golf or do whatever the hell he pleased, as long as he left the business strategy to Cameron.

Low grumbles came from around the table.

"No women? Sounds like a waste of two weeks," said Max.

Derek took a swipe at Max's head, but Max ducked. "You're whining more than you did back on the footy field."

"Piss off," said Max lazily. "Not all of us have a hot woman at home to—"

"Watch what you say about my wife," growled Derek, all two-hundred-plus pounds of muscle ready to tackle his former teammate.

"Enough," said Cameron.

The discussion was over. He trusted this group of men with his life. If he asked them to keep a low profile, they'd all do it. And so would he. Starting tomorrow.

Cameron took a gulp of his beer and scanned the

lounge to see if anyone was still watching them. He stopped on a woman sitting at the end of the bar, her eyes on him. Red lips and long brown hair in waves down her back. A silky shirt, see-through, thanks to the angle of the lights, and a black skirt riding up her thighs. She was looking, not listening, and there was something dreamy, unfocused, in her gaze. As if she were thinking through the course of her night, too.

The woman pulled her bottom lip between her teeth and looked down into her drink. Damn. How soon could he get this meeting over with?

Simon leaned in and grabbed the paper off the table in front of him, scanning it again. "So they're sending this asshole—" he pointed at the name in the middle of the page "—Jackson McAllister all the way from New York just to follow us around for two weeks?"

"What kind of wanky name is Jackson McAllister?" Max waved his hand around, almost knocking over his beer.

"The kind that will be firing all of our asses if we're not careful," said Derek.

Cameron sighed. "Look, he'll be around the office a bit, but it's really me he's supposed to follow. To see if a little public relations training can 'fix' our image. Fix my image, actually. It's my job that's on the line. The board was pretty specific on that."

Max blew out his breath. "Sorry, mate."

Cameron swallowed the bile creeping up his throat and shrugged. "So the plan is to give this dickhead a grand welcome to Sydney, show him that this is all a big misunderstanding, that we're not all drunken brawlers who like to pick up women every night, and then send him on his way back to New York."

Derek snorted. "Good luck with that."

"It's fine," said Cameron. "I can play nice for a few days. And so can you all."

Derek raised a skeptical eyebrow at Max.

"Piss off, Derek," said Max and punched him in the arm. "You were partying just as much as the rest of us before you met Laurie."

"Here's the thing," said Cameron, cutting off the exchange. "I called you here because I wanted you to know ahead of time. I'm meeting with the guy tomorrow morning, and we'll all go to dinner at Circular Quay, all nice and civil-like. But until then, you don't know anything. So you all have one last night before the ax comes down."

He looked around the table. The expressions on all three faces of his team grew into grins, as if they were each imagining what they were going to do with this night. Cameron didn't need to use his imagination. The woman was sitting right in his line of sight. Her wine was almost gone, so it was time to wrap up this meeting.

Cameron cleared his throat.

"Oh, well, thanks for the heads-up," said Max, all traces of his frown gone. He stood up and set his beer on the table. "So what are we waiting for? Who's in for the pub?"

Derek smiled. "Laurie's out until ten, so I'm up for a couple drinks. But I want to make it home by then."

Max rolled his eyes. "Me and lover boy. What about you, Simon?"

"Of course."

"And you, boss?"

Cameron eyed the bar. The woman was looking in his direction again. This time, she waited an extra beat before she lowered her long dark lashes. A good sign.

"I'm sticking around here for a while," he said. "But I'll call you if I change my mind."

"Whatever, mate." Max shook his head. "You gonna check into a room here and rent some porn for your last night of freedom?"

"Get the fuck out of here," he said, chuckling.

Cameron watched his team head out of the hotel. He took the last drink from his beer and set it down. He turned for one more look at the luscious woman at the bar. If he ended up alone tonight, he'd have plenty of material to get off on. Her skirt rode high enough to get a good look at her shapely bare legs. Was she the type who liked to ride or be ridden? Or both?

Cameron stood up and started over to the bar. He caught her gaze and held it. She squinted a little. Then her eyes widened, as if this were the last thing she expected to happen. Hmm. One of those curvy bombshells who somehow hadn't realized just how sexy she was? Even better.

As he came closer, the corners of her mouth turned up into a little smile. He slid into the stool next to hers. His legs were too long to fit under the bar, so he faced her instead.

She turned and brushed her silky hair over her shoulder. Her smile grew wider. "Hi, there."

She was American? She had one of those soft, raspy voices that was going to get him hard right here in the bar if he wasn't careful. This was getting better by the minute.

"What's your name?" he asked.

She shook her head and smiled. No names? He could do that.

"Okay," he said. "Should I start with, 'Do you come here often?'"

She gave a throaty laugh. "Is that all you got?"

Shit, this was going to be fun. He leaned closer and whispered, "Depends on what you want."

A flush crept up her slender neck and onto her cheeks. She swallowed. "Just so you know, I'm not into getting picked up at a bar."

He raised an eyebrow. "Maybe you're looking at it wrong."

"Is that right?" She gave a little snort of amusement.

He nodded. "It's all about having fun. About trying new things you might not try anywhere else. And living for the moment."

"How very philosophical," she said, crossing her arms. "Does that usually work for you?"

Cameron hung his head and laughed. "I've got a good record."

She rolled her eyes. "No wonder you're so cocky. *That* kind of guy."

"If you know my kind, then you know I love a challenge. And you've just raised the stakes, sweetheart," he said softly.

The woman took the last sip of her wine and licked her lips. She met his gaze again, and for a moment, an electric spark sizzled through him, held him there. Did she feel it, too? Her long, dark lashes fluttered.

Then the amusement was back in her smile. And maybe a hint of challenge.

"You're going to have to work a lot harder than this," she said.

Cameron rested his foot on her bar stool to get closer. "I'll work as long and hard as you want me to."

She gasped softly, and her mouth dropped for a brief moment. What was she imagining right now? Then she laughed. "Enough with the lines," she said, shaking her head.

"But they're working so well," he deadpanned. He shifted back. "You're not just a little curious?"

She hesitated, so he continued. "You know what I'm most curious about?"

She narrowed her eyes and slowly shook her head.

"I'm wondering what makes you hot," he said, lowering his voice.

As he spoke, her gaze darted down between his legs, where he was fighting a full-on erection. Maybe this wasn't such a long shot after all.

"Are you wondering how big I am?" he whispered. "What it might feel like?"

She met his gaze, and the fire sparked between them. Hell, she liked this game just as much as he did.

"Does it have any correlation with your ego?" she asked sweetly.

He quirked a brow. "You're welcome to find out for yourself." He fought another smile as her gaze landed between his legs again. Definitely interested.

"Size is overrated," she said, wrinkling her nose. "I'd rather have a man who knows how to use it."

She smelled like something delicious. Her lips were red and wet and only inches away. "What if you can have both?"

CHAPTER TWO

JACKSON MCALLISTER SWALLOWED the flutter in her throat as she stared at this man's soft, full lips. Thick black hair, deep blue eyes and a little stubble along his hard jaw. At least she thought she saw all that. So what if she couldn't actually see him clearly? Her imagination took off where her vision ended. And putting those two together, this guy was unreal. Big and built enough for even her to make out the outlines of his muscles against his black T-shirt. He was so out of her league. But just a moment ago, she could have sworn something had passed between them.

If she wanted to prove Cheater Rob wrong, now was her chance. She *did* know how to have fun in bed. And even without her contacts in, this guy looked like he was all about the best kinds of fun. He had such big... arms. Sure, he had an ego the size of this hotel, but did it matter? If she wanted to get back in the saddle, so to speak, maybe she needed someone who wasn't so concerned about his own performance.

Best of all, no one would ever know. Jackson had never set foot on this continent before today, and she had sidestepped names. What better introduction to Australia? This trip didn't allow for all the sightseeing in her little red book, so why not try her own private cultural primer? Okay, so he sounded American—she detected a slight accent on a few words—but she could make an exception in this case.

Her mother's mantra rang in her ears: *Good things come to those who wait.* Well, she had put off this kind of careless fun for long enough. And he was looking pretty good. Her mother probably hadn't meant for Jackson to apply her favorite saying in this way, which would make it all the more fun.

She reached for her little red book, tucked inside the pocket of her purse, but stopped. No, she wasn't going to add "hot sex in Sydney" to the Australia page, just so she could cross at least one item off the list. Not here, right in front of this particular tourist attraction.

Jackson bit her lip and met his gaze. He looked familiar, though she had given up any hope of recognizing anyone when she left her contacts back in her hotel room. At least her eyes weren't stinging anymore. Her glasses had gotten her down to the bar, but she'd slipped them back in their case when she sat down. And she wasn't about to pull them out to get a better look at this guy.

He gazed at her like he had all the time in the world. But she knew he was ready to get things started. And she was thinking this just might happen. A kiss couldn't hurt.

"What do you think?" he asked. "Want to see if this is as good as I think it will be?"

She glanced at his left hand. "No ring?"

He laughed. "Do I strike you as the relationship type?"

That deep, sexy voice was killing her. She rested one hand on his hard, muscular thigh. "Okay. Let's see what you've got."

She leaned forward and took his bottom lip between hers. She sucked gently and went back for more, pressing her mouth against his and licking his bottom lip this time. A rumble rose from his chest, and he took control. He slipped his tongue inside her mouth for a few lazy strokes, and he slid his large hand behind her head, pulling her closer. He teased and coaxed until she wove her hand into his thick dark hair, responding, asking for more. Easing off his chair to standing, he ran his hands over her hips as he took the kiss deeper. Harder. His erection pressed firmly against her, and she moaned a little louder than she should have.

He pulled back, and she let go of the handful of hair she was grasping. *Whoa.*

"Fuck," he muttered under his breath and sank back into his stool.

She looked up, and his eyes were closed. He shook his head a little and opened them again.

"I guess we've answered the first question," he said with a wry smile. "It'll definitely be good."

She nodded. This was already sexier than anything she'd done in a long time, and they had only kissed.

His gaze was fixed on her, and she took the opportunity to stare back. At least she tried to. He *did* look familiar. Maybe he was an actor, someone from a movie she had seen? His hair had fallen down into his face. If he were her boyfriend, she'd push it back. But he wasn't. Far from it. Which made this all the more tempting.

"Well, sweetheart," he said. "Are we going to walk away, or are we taking this to the next level?"

This was either going to be the best decision she'd ever made or the dumbest.

"I've got a room," she whispered.

He smiled. "I like your choice."

She gathered her purse and they stood up. *Good God*, he was big. What would it be like to have a man this size over her? He'd crush her if he flopped around like Cheater Rob. She frowned. No more Rob thoughts tonight.

"Can I use your mobile for a minute?" he asked.

Jackson raised an eyebrow, but he looked serious. She unlocked it and handed it over. He found the camera and took a picture of himself.

"Oooh, a commemorative photo of our evening," she said, laughing. "Thanks."

He looked down at her and sighed. "For your safety," he said drily.

Oh. Why the hell didn't she think of safety? She must be loopy on all his super-alpha pheromones.

"Can anyone access your email?"

She shrugged. "My sister, I guess."

"Then email the photo to yourself and write, 'This is who I was with tonight.'"

Well, that *was* a good idea, now that he mentioned it. She typed the message and sent it.

"Ready?" he asked.

Yep, she was definitely ready.

They managed to make it through the lobby, but when the elevator doors closed, all bets were off. He backed her against the wall for another searing kiss. He licked the seam of her mouth, and she opened, answering back with her own explorations. He found her thigh with his hand, and he slipped it under the hem of her skirt. His teeth scraped her bottom lip, and he bit down softly. His hand slid higher, and she squirmed against him. He was rock hard.

"I can feel you," she whispered. "All of you."

He smiled. "You worried?"

"Should I be?"

He didn't answer, so she reached between them and palmed him gently. His groan echoed through the elevator chamber as she stroked from base to tip, and he muttered an indecipherable string of curse words. He grabbed her hand, but the elevator dinged before he could do anything more.

Jackson stepped out and took a deep breath. She had flown from New York to Sydney today and had been awake for God knew how long. Now she was taking the world's hottest man to her hotel room for what promised to be the best sex of her life. Hopefully the jet lag wouldn't catch up with her any time soon.

They turned the corner, and she stopped in front of the first room. He swept her hair aside and kissed her neck as she fumbled with the key. But before she could open the door, his hand covered hers.

"You are on fire," he whispered in her ear. "And I want to give you more pleasure tonight than you've had in your life."

Her pulse pounded in her throat. Damn, this was unreal.

"But if you don't like something," he continued, "just say stop and I'll back off. No matter what we're in the middle of. Got it?"

She nodded.

"Good."

He took her key and pushed it in the lock, and the door swung open. He was right behind her, crowding her. As soon as the door closed, he turned her around and pressed her back against the door with the weight of his body. She cupped his jaw in her hands and pulled his mouth toward hers. His lips came down on hers, hungry and insistent. His grip tightened around her waist, but he pulled back.

"What do you want?" he growled.

"An orgasm, please?" she squeaked.

Jackson covered her mouth. Did she really just say that?

He leaned his forehead against the door, and his shoulders shook with silent laughter. "Yeah, I got that," he finally said.

He straightened up and met her gaze. His smile

slowly shifted from amusement back to searing lust. He ran his hands up and down her waist in slow, sensual sweeps. "I mean, what do you like?" he said, his voice low and gruff. "This can be as gentle or as rough as you want it."

The word *rough* sang through her body. What did he imagine when he said it?

"How do you want this to be?" she hedged.

His eyes widened, and he smiled. "I wasn't expecting that answer." He rubbed the stubble on his chin. "I want this to be the best night of your life. I want you to wake up missing the feeling of my cock in you."

A rush of heat flooded her. His words turned her on just as much as his ravenous kisses. Jackson had no idea what to say.

He put his hand back on her waist. "How 'bout we start with this," he said before his lips brushed the base of her jaw.

She swallowed and nodded.

His tongue was soft and teasing. She ran her hands over the thick muscles of his arms. He found the edge of her shirt and tugged it up. She pulled it over her head, and his breath caught. "Mmm... That bra is perfect."

She smiled. See-through lace. Her nipples poked out, hard, begging for attention. "Glad you like it."

"Hell, yeah." He cupped her breasts and rubbed his thumbs over the peaks. She moaned, and his erection throbbed hard against her.

"Turn around," he said.

She faced the door, and he unclasped the bra, pushing the straps over her shoulders. She let it fall to the floor. Her breasts were heavy, and they tingled in the cool air. Would he play with them?

He knelt down behind her and unzipped her skirt. Oh. He slid his hands under the material and pushed the skirt over her hips. It fell to the floor, too, and she stood in nothing but her panties.

He didn't touch at first. His breath came in gentle puffs on her back. "Lace again," he said, running his hands over the material.

A little gasp escaped from her lips. He kissed the small of her back and eased the panties down, as well.

She was naked and giddy, but his caresses slowed. His hand trailed down her spine, and when he came to her rear, one finger continued. Then he stopped at the most daring place of all.

She shivered.

"You ever played here?" he asked softly.

Jackson hesitated. She hadn't, but she was definitely curious. Should she say yes, just to see what it was like? She shook her head.

"Okay," he said, and his finger trailed lower. "Then we'll play here."

His finger teased her clit, and then it was gone. He turned her around and tugged off his own shirt. He undid the front of his pants, and her mouth fell open as he reached in to give himself a long, hard stroke.

He looked up at her darkly. "First I want to lick you, and then I want to fuck you hard. How does that sound?"

"Like the most erotic thing I've ever heard," Jackson blurted. Shit. That had slipped out.

He gave her a hungry smile. "Okay, sweetheart. Put your leg over my shoulder."

She lifted her leg and rested it on the hard wall of muscles along his back. She was so exposed and wound up that she wasn't sure how long she could stand like this.

He wrapped his hands around her hips and buried his face in her. He ran his tongue along her inner thigh until he reached her clit. Then he sucked hard. Pleasure shot through her body. She cried out and her head fell back. So he did it again. His tongue traveled over a new spot, exploring, learning her responses. But he went slowly, so slowly. Jackson tangled her hands into his hair, begging him for more. Shudders of heat rushed through her, more and more intense each time. He groaned when she responded, but he didn't stop; he found new places to lick and suck, bringing her closer and closer until she fell back against the wall. Want turned to need. Then a bolt of ecstasy exploded inside, and she came in white-hot spasms.

She panted, trying to hold herself up. It was too much. He caught her in his arms and brought her down to the floor against him. He held her like that until her breaths slowed.

"That was amazing," she whispered.

"We can do it as many times as you want," he said.

His pants had fallen open, and his erection strained through the last layer of clothing between them. She kissed his shoulder and leaned back, taking in the sight of him. "When do you get naked?" she asked.

He put his hands on his knees and stood up in front of her. Oh. Now. She slid his pants down his legs. He toed off his shoes and kicked his pants aside. Jackson rose on her knees and fingered the waistband of his boxers.

She swallowed. Finally she was going to get a look at what promised to be the most impressive display she had ever seen, with or without glasses. Taking a deep breath, she inched down his waistband. His tip glistened in front of her. She tugged his boxers down farther, and he bent down to help her. He stepped out, and she got a nice, long view of him. *Long* being the operative word.

"Oh, my," she whispered.

He laughed, and their eyes met. His smile faded. For one quiet moment, neither of them moved. The scene was outrageously erotic. She was naked on her knees, with his enormous cock bobbing in front of her, but there was something else, too. A different kind of spark between them, something that made this scene even better.

Whoa, girl. Way too deep for casual sex.

She looked away from his hypnotic blue eyes and began to explore. She traced him slowly from tip to base. His breaths quickened as she stroked and squeezed him, and he rocked into her touch.

He leaned forward to help her up, and he nodded to the bed.

"You ready?" All the smoothness in his voice was gone.

"Yes."

He reached for his jeans and pulled out his wallet. The wrapper crackled as he tore it off and rolled on the condom. She was beyond caring that she was staring at him with open lust.

"Turn around," he said softly, and she did.

He pressed up behind her, his erection hard against her back. Leaning over her, he moved her hair to one side and gently bit her earlobe. He reached around and squeezed her breasts. Oh, yes. He liked that, too. He played with her nipples, squeezing harder until she gasped.

"I want you from behind," he said, his harsh breaths in her ear.

She nodded and crawled onto the bed, and he followed, never letting go of her. Spreading her legs farther with his knees, he slid his erection along every sensitive place. He teased her and played, and she moved to find new angles of pleasure. His tip pressed at her entrance, and her body yielded to him. With a low groan, he pushed himself all the way in.

She cried out, and he stilled, his fingers flexing hard on her hips.

"You okay?" he said through gritted teeth.

"Yes." She could barely get out the sound. Everything felt full, and she squirmed to adjust.

"Hold on," he bit out, and he held her in place. He pulled out slowly and sank back in hard.

A wild moan escaped her.

"You like that, sweetheart?" he growled.

"Yes," she whispered.

In response, he did it again. Then again and again, pulling out and driving back in. Each time, she sank back on her knees, searching for more. Her body felt lighter as the pleasure built, threatening to explode inside her. His thrusts grew harder and more frantic.

"I—I'm going to..." she stuttered just as the pleasure flooded her once more, the long spasms racking her body. Her arms collapsed as wave after luscious wave of heat rolled through her.

His hips crashed against her, driving deeper, and he came with a torn roar. His big body fell over hers, and he rested his chest on her back. She collapsed in a boneless, sated heap.

Moments passed. He eased down onto the bed and shifted her to his side. His heart pumped in overdrive against her back, and his breath was heavy over her as he stroked her hair softly. She couldn't see him, but he was everywhere, all around her, holding her close. Like his body belonged there, right against hers.

Wow. Just wow. This was what sex could be like? It was probably better than anything she'd ever have again. If she weren't so tired, maybe she'd ask to do it one more time.

"My God," she whispered. "If I had known that one-night stands were this good, I would have started doing this a long time ago."

He didn't laugh at her joke. He didn't answer. He smoothed her hair once more and kissed her on the top of her head. His lips stayed there for an extra beat, and then they were gone.

He rolled away from her and wandered around the room, probably looking for somewhere to put the condom. He bent down and untangled his clothes from the heap on the floor. Was he leaving now? He stepped into his boxers and pulled on his jeans. He picked up his shirt, but he didn't put it on. Instead, he sat down on the bed right next to her. It dipped under his weight.

Jackson was still wearing nothing, and she climbed under the covers. Her whole body felt heavy and slow. The jet lag was setting in hard. Her eyes fluttered closed, and she fought to open them again.

He pulled the blanket over her shoulders and studied her, but she couldn't make out his expression.

"I think I should go," he said.

"Okay," she said. "Um, thanks, I guess."

His teeth flashed in a smile.

"You're welcome, sweetheart. I'll think of you often when I'm alone in bed."

Jackson smiled. "Likewise."

He stood up and headed for the door. When it clicked behind him, she closed her eyes and fell asleep.

CHAPTER THREE

CAMERON WOKE UP with a hand on his cock. Damn. It was *his* hand, not the hand of the hot-as-hell woman who had featured in his dream. The woman with a smart, sexy mouth, a nice round ass and no name.

He was already hard as a rock and halfway there, so he slipped down his boxers and closed his eyes. Last night in the shower, he had gotten himself off to all the things he wanted to do with her nice round ass. This morning he'd dedicate to that smart, sexy mouth.

His fantasy began just like she had the night before. She'd touched him with her hands, but this time she'd use her lips and her tongue. Yes, those eager lashes of her tongue. In his dream, instead of walking out, he stayed for another round. He grasped her long, luscious hair in both hands and guided himself in and out of her mouth, thrusting deeper, while she stared up at him with those deep green eyes. Fuck.

Cameron gave himself a few last hard strokes and came with a loud groan. He collapsed back on his bed, panting. As the haze of pleasure faded, he shook his head and frowned. When was the last time he'd woken himself up like that? At least he should be able to lie back for a few more minutes of satisfaction. Instead he was restless. And irritable. And still thinking about her comment from the night before.

If I had known that one-night stands were this good, I would have started doing this a long time ago.

What the hell? One-night stands weren't that good. In fact, Cameron couldn't think of one that had come close. But when he opened his mouth to tell her, he'd stopped. If he said that the night went far beyond any one-night stand, then what? Starting today, he was supposed to keep his dick in his pants. There was no hope for a repeat performance. So he'd gotten dressed and walked out of the woman's room instead.

He had told her he wanted her to remember it as the best night of her life. But by the time he left her, he'd reconsidered. If they were that good together on the first try, what would happen when they really started exploring each other?

No. That couldn't happen. And he wasn't about to ruin the memories of that night with sappy shit that didn't matter anyway.

Cameron kicked off his covers, took a few long strides to the bathroom and slammed the door. He turned the shower on punishingly cold, hoping for a distraction. Because the more he thought about this no-women situation, the madder he got.

This PR bullshit the board had arranged was no longer just a nuisance. Last night it meant that he had had to walk away from the best sex in a long time. Maybe that woman was staying in Sydney for a while. Hell, maybe she even lived close by and they could have gone on fucking like that for days. Instead he was making a mess of himself in his boxers right before going to meet with that fucker Jackson McAllister.

Screw Harlan Blackmore and his board. This was the last straw. He had been waiting for the right moment to take control away from them for years, and this was it. His grandfather had built this business years ago to give veterans from his unit a purpose after the Vietnam War. It was the bond of the teams that made his grandfather's business strong, not the latest PR. Okay, so his team may have gotten a little careless with their public image, but hiring a babysitter to shadow and report on Cameron smacked of his father's dirty tactics. Harlan had latched on to this situation and intervened as a show of force. There wasn't too much bad press at this point. Wouldn't a warning from the board have sufficed? Then Cameron could've dealt with his team on his own terms. He needed to show his father and the board just how far up their asses their heads were. And the best way to do that would be to send Jackson McAllister home looking like an idiot.

He shut off the water and toweled off, then he strode into his walk-in closet and reached for a pair of jeans. One leg into them, he stopped and cursed. Probably should wear a suit for this meeting.

By the time he climbed the dock off his building, he still wasn't thinking clearly. His boat floated peacefully in its berth. Maybe a good fast ride across the harbor would help. Buying that boat was the best decision he'd made since he moved to Sydney. No crowds, no traffic, everything in sight. Those trips across the water every day were the few moments he didn't have to be on guard. Cameron nodded at the captain and took a seat. He enjoyed this type of travel...and he knew from his army days there were worse ways to get around. Hell, after the plane crash he'd been through, no one could fault him for being picky in that regard.

He pushed those thoughts aside.

If he'd learned anything in the military, it was just how much better things went with a clear plan. And judging from the start of his morning, he was in no state to come up with a good one. But in this pissy mood, any plan was better than none. As the boat passed under the Harbour Bridge, he sent an email to his team. Tonight at dinner they'd figure out Jackson McAllister's weak spots. Tomorrow they'd figure out how to use them.

But planning didn't help. When he walked through the glass doors into the Blackmore Inc. office, his mood was just as dark.

"Good morning, Mr. Blackmore."

He bit out a greeting to Chloe, the receptionist, and headed for his office.

"Mr. Blackmore," she called after him. "Jackson McAllister is waiting for you in the small conference room."

He grunted but didn't turn around. What the hell? The guy wasn't supposed to be there for another thirty minutes. Cameron changed direction and headed straight for the conference room. He was going to have to tell that fuckwit to come back later.

He burst through the door and came to a full stop. In one of the chairs he saw a woman, not a man. The rear of a woman, to be specific, turned away, bending over a mess of papers on the floor. What the—

"Sorry. Just a moment," came a voice from under the round table.

A voice that awakened his entire body. He gave himself a little shake. What the fuck was going on?

"I got the time mixed up…" The woman rose with a pile of papers and turned. And froze.

"Oh," she whispered. "Damn."

It was her. The hot-as-hell woman. His body had known the moment she spoke, and now his mind finally registered it. Her lips were pale, not red, and she was wearing glasses, but this only added to her appeal. She had her long, silky hair up in a bun. He already knew the feeling of a fistful of that hair, and he had gotten himself off to what those lips would look like around his—

"What are you doing here?" he barked.

The words came out as more of an accusation than a question. Lust must have short-circuited his brain because he still couldn't figure out how the hell this woman had ended up at his office building.

But as he glared across the room at her, all the wonder disappeared from her expression. She took off her glasses and blinked at him a couple times before putting them back on. She narrowed her eyes and pressed her lips together into a tight smile. She stood up and stuck out her hand for a handshake.

"Jackson McAllister," she said. "The board warned me about your growling."

Cameron screwed his eyes shut and rubbed his forehead. He opened his eyes again, but nothing changed. The same woman was still glaring at him.

"What the hell?" he whispered. "You're not a man."

Jackson dropped her hand and raised her eyebrows. "I think you and I already established that last night, Mr. Blackmore," she said drily. "And you're supposed to have a beard."

So... *She* was Jackson McAllister. The person the board had sent to rein in him and his team. Or try to. And he had already given her an eye-opening welcome. Cameron rubbed his temples.

"But Jackson's a man's name," he muttered to himself.

She shook her head slowly. "Why do I feel like I'm back in elementary school?"

"I'm long past elementary school, Ms. McAllister," he snapped. "I think we established that last night, too."

Her face betrayed no emotion, but a deep flush crept up her neck. Which brought him right back to the place his mind absolutely should not go now. The last time those cheeks reddened like that was—

Shit. What was he supposed to do now? Pull out a chair for her all gentleman-like? Ignore the fact that he had just had mind-bending sex with her less than twelve hours ago? He huffed out a breath and sank into his own chair at the table.

He crossed his arms and leaned back, scrambling to get a handle on the situation. Wait. He'd had no idea who she was last night, but had she known who he was? Was this part of some larger scheme to "tame" him? He nearly snarled at the thought. It sure as hell hadn't felt that way. And when he walked into the conference room, she'd looked just as confused as he had felt. But he couldn't rule it out.

"You had to know it was me last night," he said slowly. "Didn't the board give you photos or something?"

Jackson rolled her eyes. "I didn't spend hours gazing at your profile, if that's what you mean. You had a beard in most of them, and last night I took my contacts out because my eyes were killing me."

Well, those glasses gave her an innocent-but-naughty look that would turn him on right here if he kept thinking about it. Fighting for calm, he said, "Screw it. Let's do this."

Her eyes snapped up to meet his, and another blush washed over her cheeks. Wait—did he just catch her staring at his biceps? She sat down quickly in her chair and smoothed her skirt over her legs. She grabbed the files she had just collected from the floor and cleared her throat.

"I'm here to give you a boost of intensive public relations support," she said. "I'll be looking at every detail of your day and coming up with a plan for improvement."

"Any suggestions so far?" The comment slipped out before he could think better of it. And fuck if she didn't lick her lips before *she* could think better of it.

But the glossy look in her eyes quickly switched back to a glare. "The board wants a detailed report," she said sharply. "And there I'll make suggestions for the future."

All his retorts faded. He hadn't missed the board's veiled threat. If Cameron didn't run his company the Harlan Blackmore way, someone else would. But he hadn't missed Jackson's threat, either. And the glare she still fixed on him said the same thing: *Don't mess with me.*

Cameron ran a hand through his hair and blew out a breath. "How the hell do you propose we make this work, Jackson?"

She let out a little sigh. Her eyes softened, and she pushed her glasses up her nose. For a moment, she looked just as mixed up about the situation as he was. But when she spoke again, her voice was steady and all business.

"We just forget about last night and do our jobs," she said. "I'm over it. You're a big boy. You can get past it, too, can't you?"

She knew just how much of a big boy he was, but now wasn't the time to point this out.

"I think I can manage that," he said drily. "Let's get to work."

She opened a file and pushed it toward him. He picked up the printouts of newspaper articles and photos one by one. He had seen most of them before. They featured various members of his team with different women from different jobs. Most of them weren't remarkable. He could see her point, too—he did have a beard in most of them.

"These are clients," he said.

She picked up one of Max and a high-profile actress. He was whispering something in her ear, and if the sultry smile on her face was any indication, she was ready for him to do a lot more.

"He looks more like a male escort than a bodyguard," she said.

Cameron took the photo back. "What can I say? He's good at his job."

He continued through the pile. He found a photo of himself coming out of a pub with two women, one on each side. He was talking to one, and the other was holding on to his bicep, her mouth next to his ear.

His gaze flicked up to meet hers. "That's not what it looks like."

"Let me guess," she said sweetly. "You're good at your job, too?"

He rested his gaze on her. "I am good at my job." He added softly, "And aside from that, I prefer to enjoy women one at a time."

She didn't answer, but she lost some of the hardness in her expression. What was going on in her mind right now? Did she like more than one man at a time?

The idea boiled in him. Hell, no. But that was the last thing he should be getting upset about right now. Nothing was going to happen between them again. Not a bloody thing.

He leafed through the rest of the photos and articles until he came to one that made him stop. It was a single photo with no words. There was no other indication of where it came from except for a long web address at the top of the page.

"Where did you find this?" he snapped.

Jackson took the paper from his hand and studied it. "I'm not sure about this one. We ran a search on the company's name and all your team members' names and printed out everything we came across from this last year. Why are you asking?"

"That's not a client. That's Derek Latu with his wife, Laurie."

"He's married?" she asked, as if this were the last thing she expected to hear.

"Very happily. Surprised?" Cameron gave her a pointed look. "I told you this shit doesn't tell the whole story." He gestured to the photo. "Yes, he has a wife, but she stays far away from any press. She's had some stalker issues in the past."

"Oh." Jackson looked at the web address again. "It doesn't come from anywhere I recognize."

"That's what worries me." He looked at the photo once more and set it aside on the table. "Can I keep this? I want to show it to Derek."

Jackson nodded and gathered together the rest of the clippings.

"Whether these photos represent jobs or—" she waved her hand around as if she were searching for the right words "—or other encounters is beside the point from a PR perspective. This is going to become the Blackmore Inc. image if you don't make some changes."

"Says my father," finished Cameron with more than a little bitterness.

He thought she'd deny it, but she didn't. Instead, Jackson gave him a look that was almost sympathetic. "Yes. But it's important for the company, too. Especially if you're saying we're not seeing the whole story."

"Even though the Australian division of Blackmore Inc. is doing better now than it was when my father ran the show?"

"Yep. Probably even because of it."

Cameron sighed. Well, at least they were on the same page in that regard.

"All right," he grumbled. "What's next?"

Jackson flipped through her file to the first pages, biting her lip. Cameron couldn't keep his eyes off those plump, soft lips that had promised him so much pleasure the night before. What would it feel like if she—

"I just want to make sure I have all the basics," she said, looking up at him. Her eyes rounded.

Shit. Were his thoughts so transparent?

Jackson's eyes skittered away and she cleared her throat. "You and three other men make up your main team for on-the-ground security. Max Jensen comes from a prominent ranching family in Australia, and you two were roommates at Princeton. He's the one with his photo on the front page of the papers."

Cameron scowled. "He's also the one who brought both clients and credibility into the Australian market when I took over. His family's name goes a long way down here."

She nodded and jotted a few notes before looking back up. "After you both graduated, he returned to Australia and played rugby, where he met Derek Latu. You enlisted in the army."

Cameron gave a dry laugh. "Much to my father's dismay."

"But not your grandfather's, I'm assuming," she said. "Following his path, the way he built this company."

Very good, Jackson McAllister. He crossed his arms and waited.

"You and Simon Rodriguez were in the same unit," she continued, "and when you both returned, you hired him."

Cameron nodded.

Jackson flipped the page and scanned it. "Not long after, your grandfather put you in charge of Australia and moved your father back to New York." She raised her gaze to his. "I'd imagine your father wouldn't have taken that very well."

Cameron didn't answer. This woman was good. She had done her background work and read between the lines. But even as sympathetic as she had sounded, he couldn't forget for a minute she was working for the board. Not for him.

Jackson looked back down at the pages in her file. "You and Simon Rodriguez came to Sydney, brought Max Jensen and Derek Latu on board, and the four of you started to rethink the company's strategy."

"That's about it," he said.

Jackson looked at him for an extra beat, her green eyes searching his. Then she stuffed her files into her bag. "Let's take a quick tour around the office so I can get a feel for what goes on here. Then we'll look at your schedule. I want to spend the first couple of days getting an idea of what you're doing now."

"Fine," he said, grabbing his briefcase.

Cameron stood up and took a deep breath. He'd just had a conversation with her and hadn't once thought about sex. Well, not for the last part of the conversation, anyway. Progress. He could do this.

She gathered her things, and he gestured to let her go first out of the conference room. Big mistake. Because now he was right behind her with a clear view of that nice round rear he had so appreciated last night. Her skirt was longer today, but it had a slit up the back that got him wondering. How high would it slide up her legs? She was wearing silky stockings. Were they the kind that went all the way up, or did they stop somewhere out of sight and leave the tops of her delicious thighs bare?

Shit. He turned his head and looked down the hall at anything he could find—the plants, the sprinkler system, the lights—anything but the spectacular view of Jackson calling his name.

She turned around. "Which way?"

"I'll lead," he growled. He turned down the hall and headed for the elevators. *Say something, you fuckwit.* Cameron mentally shook himself. "It's just the four of us principals, a couple of admins and some meeting rooms on this floor. The other three guys aren't in the office right now. We'll need to go downstairs for the rest of the company."

He pushed the elevator call button.

"The floor below us is where most of the logistics people sit as well as the teams under each of us four," he said. "Clients want all sorts of security these days, and since I took over the Sydney business, we've broadened according to what the companies here need."

The elevator doors opened, and they stepped in. *Just keep talking.*

"Derek and Max both head up on-the-ground security teams, and Simon is developing our surveillance branch. A lot of the work we do can be carried out in the office, but we work as a team when jobs require more specialized security. That's just for the very high-end clients, and the four of us are on-site for those jobs. Those are the ones that you see in the photos."

Cameron cleared his throat and shoved his hands in his pockets. The doors opened.

"We're two floors down now, in our IT department," he said. "With the kind of security we do, we can't out-source anything."

He led her around, introducing her to employees at all levels. He knew everyone in the company. He had to if he was going to entrust so many people's safety to them.

Jackson smiled and shook everyone's hands, remembering names and asking questions. He had to admit she was really good. But as they made their way through accounting, her eyes began to droop. She must be tired.

"You want to take a break?" he asked.

Jackson took off her glasses and rubbed her eyes. "I think I've seen enough to get us started. Let's head back upstairs."

He led the way back to the elevators. On the ride up, she looked more and more tired by the minute. They finally came to the door of his office, and he opened it for her.

"Oh, my God," she said breathlessly, walking up to the tall glass windows. "That's the Harbour Bridge."

He started toward her, ready to point out the Opera House, but he froze as his mind kicked back into gear. He was not going to stand next to her and breathe in the warm scent of her hair. They needed to get back to business. "Yes," he grunted, trying not to look in her direction.

He hauled an extra chair over to the opposite side of his desk, then sank into his. She sat down, too, and he pulled up his schedule for the day before swiveling his monitor toward her.

"No meetings this morning?" she asked.

He shook his head. "Moved them all. I wasn't sure what you'd have in mind."

She bent over to look closer at his computer screen, giving him a flash down her button-up shirt. Luscious, round breasts strained against a lacy pink bra. Luscious, round breasts that he spent far too little time on last night. That he would never play with again. He forced his gaze back to the computer screen.

"What's this?" she asked, pointing to the lunch hour block.

"I work out at our gym every day. It's a few floors down from here. Below IT."

"Oh."

"You gonna observe me there, too?" he asked, fighting a grin.

She caught her lip between her teeth. "I'd check out everything with any other client."

"You're welcome to watch." Cameron gave her a lazy smile and added, "If the board insists."

A touch of pink stained her cheeks. "Maybe another day."

"Suit yourself," he said smoothly. "I'll probably be on the phone most of the afternoon checking in with clients. And then we'll meet the rest of the team for dinner tonight."

"They don't come into the office every day?"

"Most days I'm here, and they come in when they're not on security jobs." Thankfully, as CEO, Cameron had a good excuse not to travel—neglecting the daily operations was how his father got the Sydney office into trouble in the first place. The prominent clients in Sydney kept business booming, and his teammates could handle operations farther afield, if they came up. His aversion to flying wasn't exactly good for the business, long-term, but he'd figure that out at some point. "Today the guys are looking at one of the local venues where we're providing security for a high-profile client, a politician. You'll hear the details in this week's meeting."

"Okay," she said, stifling a yawn.

He raised an eyebrow. "This job's already boring you? I told you, our business is a lot more ordinary than your photos suggest."

She shook her head. "It's not that. The jet lag is killing me."

Her eyelids sank for a moment and then snapped back open. He saw an opportunity, and he took it.

"Listen, why don't you take a taxi back to your hotel for a few hours and catch up on some sleep," he said. "Like I said, I'll just be around the office answering messages and talking to clients."

She frowned. "Probably not a good idea on my first day."

"You won't miss anything," he said. "I promise I won't get into any trouble while you're gone."

Her eyelids drooped again. "I don't know... I had planned to cover a bit more."

"We're meeting the team for dinner at seven, so I'll come by your room around six and take you there."

"Okay, maybe you're right. I probably won't be productive like this, anyway," she said, suppressing another yawn. "But I can't miss that meeting."

"I won't let you."

Jackson nodded. "See you tonight, then." She grabbed her bag and he couldn't help noticing the sway of her hips as she walked out the door.

Once she disappeared, Cameron breathed a long sigh of relief. Thank God that was over. And he had just bought himself some time to get his head on straight.

It was only after Jackson was long gone that he realized his mistake. If he was going to forget that last night ever happened, he shouldn't be anywhere near her hotel room.

CHAPTER FOUR

JACKSON WOKE UP to the sound of chimes. She sat up and scanned the room. Her phone alarm flashed in the darkness. Oh, right. The Sydney hotel room. The one she had invited Cameron Blackmore back to for sex last night.

Nice move.

She reached for her phone on the nightstand and shut off the alarm. Stretching, she flopped back onto the bed. After six hours of sleep, the fog was finally lifting off her thoughts.

Which was a good thing because Cameron would be knocking on her door soon.

She rolled out of bed, washed her face and squeezed back into business attire, muttering to herself through the whole process. What the hell was she thinking last night? Actually she knew exactly what she'd been thinking: this guy is unbelievable. Scorching. Tempting enough to have a little of that fun Rob thought she was constitutionally incapable of. The kind of fun she had never let herself have.

Just one night indulging in one of those "good things" she was long overdue for, and where did that get her? She managed to find the one man in Sydney she absolutely should not have sex with, under any circumstance. She was supposed to be fixing his reputation, not succumbing to it. She doubted the board would praise her thorough investigation skills in this area.

Jackson reached for her purse and pulled out her little red book. She flipped through the worn pages until she found the one labeled Sydney. The last item she had written was Manly Beach. She grabbed a pencil and wrote underneath, "Hot sex in Sydney." And then crossed it out. At least something good should come out of this mess.

Damn Cameron Blackmore and his deep voice and his stupid muscles he'd caught her staring at this morning. Who the hell had biceps you could see through a business shirt? And damn her own traitorous body. This morning she'd pictured office fantasies she didn't even know she had. The kinds of fantasies she should absolutely not be thinking about right before a dinner meeting with his team. The kind her career-oriented mind tried hard to avoid.

Shit. And now he was coming to her room? No.

Jackson stuffed the little red book back into her purse and grabbed her files. She leafed through them until she came to Cameron Blackmore's contact information, then sent him a text.

Meet me in the lobby.

Good. Maybe she could get this whole crazy first twenty-four hours in Sydney under control. And hope

Cameron Blackmore didn't figure out that she was probably more at risk of losing her job than he was if anyone found out.

Jackson exhaled loudly and looked at the clock. Enough time to check her messages. She opened her laptop and got to work, reading through the updates from her other clients, responding to Kyle's questions. Luckily, Kyle was a brilliant assistant, much more on top of things than any other twenty-three-year-old she had worked with before. Jackson's shoulders sank in relief. No fires to put out.

She hovered her cursor over the last unopened message, debating whether or not to click on it. She couldn't ignore a message from her own mother, could she? Okay, she'd done it once or twice in the past, but she was in a different country. Maybe her mother was actually worried. Or excited to hear about her first trip to another continent. Right.

She sighed and clicked on the message. Just as she suspected. No *Just checking in to see if you're okay.* No *You're in Sydney! I'm so proud of you.* Instead, her mother had sent a link to her sister's latest blog post featuring the twins. The two-year-olds were feeding each other her sister's latest homemade baby food creation. Okay, it was cute. Very cute. She could almost hear Marcello and Marco's laughter as they stuffed each other's mouths full, dripping all over the expensive tile floors of Jami and Fabio's Brooklyn town house. But Jami wouldn't worry about that—the maid would clean up later. Her sister would be enjoying the moment, enjoying her domestic bliss.

Unlike Jackson, Jami had managed the seemingly impossible task of living up to all their mother's expectations. She had a faithful husband, adorable kids, a big house and a successful career. For extra-credit bonus, Jami was so damn nice and good-natured. Her sister really was happy, and Jackson admired that, even if it wasn't quite the kind of happiness she was looking for. Jami had survived a type-A mother, a philandering father and their inevitably calamitous divorce relatively unscathed. Jackson? Well, she had survived. Unscathed? Debatable.

At the end of the message, her mother hadn't forgotten to add her favorite saying: "Good things come to those who wait." Thanks, Mom. Really subtle. As if Jackson were just killing time in Sydney while waiting for the rest of the things on her mother's success checklist to fall into place. She was on her own path… or, rather, she was on a ten-year plan to get onto her own path.

She gritted her teeth and hit Reply.

Thanks for sending. Marcello and Marco are adorable, as always. PS I'm having a great time in Sydney.

For once, she was grateful her mother would never think to ask about the nature of her "great time." Jackson closed her laptop and headed for the bathroom once more, pushing her mother out of her mind. She was finally in another country, a place where people went about life differently, thought about things differently. What would it be like to live another life, just for a while? That question was what had sparked her dreams of traveling long ago, when her parents were at their worst. But now traveling was more about adventure than escape, though an evening with Cameron Blackmore had certainly given her an X-rated perspective on what another life could feel like. She put on her makeup and practiced her cool, business-only smile in the mirror. She had faced sexy, built men before. She could do this.

Jackson browsed her shoe selection. Flats for walking, or heels to combat the height difference between mammoth Cameron and her? She frowned. Cameron wasn't making any wardrobe decisions based on her. No reason for her to do so for him, either.

She grabbed her flats, put them on and headed for the hotel room door. She swung it open and stepped out. And crashed into a large, solid body.

She heard an "oof," and strong arms closed around her before she fell to the ground.

Cameron.

For a moment, neither of them moved. His arms encircled her and she breathed in his warm, musky scent. God, he smelled good. She softened into him...

What the hell was she doing?

Jackson scrambled away. "You were supposed to meet me in the lobby," she snapped.

A look of realization crossed his face. "I wasn't sure who that message was from."

"You often get messages from women who want to meet you in the lobby?"

He opened his mouth to answer, but she cut him off. "Let's just go."

Jackson brushed by him and headed for the elevator. She reached the doors first and pressed the button. He shifted as they waited in silence. Was Cameron dreading the ride in this particular enclosed space, too? He loomed next to her, his bulky frame distractingly *there*.

The doors opened, and she didn't wait for any chivalrous gestures. She walked in and pressed the button for the lobby. The doors closed. She stole a glance at Cameron. He looked oblivious to her presence.

Damn him. How could he ignore what they had done together in this elevator less than twenty-four hours ago? And then there was the sex. Really, really good sex. She had never believed in all that "men are from Mars" crap, but for the first time, she wondered if men really were fundamentally different from women. Because as hard as she tried, she couldn't just turn off her reaction to him. And he could clearly turn off his.

The elevator dinged, and Jackson stomped out. She started for the lobby doors, not bothering to check if Cameron was following.

"Jackson?"

She stopped and turned around. "What?"

He caught up with her and stopped way too close for her current state of mind. Crap. Stepping farther away meant showing him just how poorly she was handling the "casual" part of casual sex. So she stayed put and wiped all traces of lust from her face. She hoped.

Over six feet of suit and muscle hovered only inches away. She tipped up her chin and met his gaze. Cameron was looking down at her with unexpected softness.

"We're not going to get through dinner like this," he said. His voice resonated inside her, quiet and intimate.

Jackson bit her lip. "You mean *I'm* not going to get through dinner. You seem to be well-practiced at this."

Cameron's eyes hardened. "You don't know anything about me."

"You're right," she said. "And you know nothing about me."

Jackson frowned. Maybe she was being a little harsh, but the gist of this conversation was right on. They knew nothing about each other. He didn't know about Cheater Rob and his "sensitive" dick or her ten-year plan or how much work it took to get this job or anything else that had landed her here in Sydney for what was becoming a nightmare assignment. Their night together was supposed to be about letting go, about fun.

And she certainly did let go and have fun with Cameron. Now why the hell couldn't she just move on and stop drooling every time he was in sight?

Still, it wasn't his fault that she was temperamentally incapable of just having a fling. They were working together. She had to stop snapping at him.

Jackson took a deep breath. "Look, this has all been a bit much for me. We made a mistake, and there's nothing to do about it but move on." She gave him a smile she hoped looked confident. "I'll be fine at dinner."

The corners of his mouth tipped down, but he didn't say anything.

"Are you ready?" she asked.

"Yeah."

They headed out of the lobby and onto the street. As the warm air hit her, some of the tension eased. While New York was cold and gray in November, Sydney's summer was just coming into full swing. They came to the street corner, and a warm, gentle breeze blew from the direction of the water.

"The restaurant's not too far," said Cameron. "You okay walking?"

"Of course," she said and stepped off the curb to cross.

A large, warm arm wrapped around her waist and pulled her back just as a car swerved around the corner. Her breath caught in her throat. The driver honked his horn, and Cameron gave the guy the finger. He held her against the hard muscles of his chest for an extra beat.

"Look right, sweetheart," he whispered in her ear. "We drive on the other side of the road down here, re-member?"

Right. She had managed to make it through the previous twenty-four hours without stepping in front of a car, but with a giant distraction named Cameron Blackmore standing next to her, her brain was apparently having trouble multitasking.

"Thanks," she mumbled. "Maybe you should lead."

He chuckled and released her. She straightened up. *Get it together, girl.* She was about to meet Cameron's team. She gave herself a little shake and tried to focus on the scenery.

Like in New York, tall glass facades mingled with older stone and brick buildings, but the Sydney streets felt cleaner. The whole city felt cleaner and brighter. It was rush hour, and a steady flow of people poured out of the offices and stores onto stone-laid sidewalks. Wow. She was actually in Australia.

Thank God she hadn't worn heels. Even flats were pressing on her toes. "Not too far" clearly meant something entirely different in Australian. Or maybe it was the fact that she took two steps for every one of Cameron's.

Jackson slowed when the harbor came into view.

"This is Circular Quay," Cameron said, pointing at the ferry terminal. "We're going to meet the team at a place out along the water."

Jackson looked where he was pointing out into the harbor. Boats moved slowly through the water, and behind them, the Sydney Opera House peeked out among the buildings. She reached into her purse and pulled out her little red book. She flipped through the pages until she felt Cameron's stare. Wait. Her most recent addition to the list was not exactly the message she wanted to send right now. She stuffed it back into her bag and pretended to look at the harbor. It worked. Cameron crossed the street, and she followed.

But did she write "visit Sydney Opera House" or had

she wanted to see a performance there? Probably the former, since her teenage self wouldn't have had much interest in operas or plays. Did seeing the building from a distance count? Nah. Someday she'd find the time to stay in Sydney for a month or two and do it properly.

But since she'd moved out of Rob's apartment, her rent had doubled. Which had turned a five-year plan into a ten-year plan. So for now, she'd have to soak up as much of the city as she could from afar. With Cameron Blackmore at her side. Which, all things considered, might be ideal under any other circumstance but this.

They walked along the water's edge. She stole a look at Cameron and found that he was studying her.

"You were good with everyone at the office today," he said. "Impressive."

Jackson smiled. "Thanks. I like my job."

"What do you like about it?"

"I can do a lot in just a couple weeks, and that feels good," she said. "Most companies just need to get on the right track."

He looked genuinely interested, so she continued.

"Before I came here I was in California," she said. "This company and its union had been in negotiations that turned sour, and that got lots of press. But when they reached an agreement, both the company and the workers wanted some good PR."

"Did your boost work?"

Jackson nodded. "It did. And they're still following the post-intervention plan I made, which is always a good sign."

He was quiet, and she was perfectly happy to just take in her surroundings. The ferries and smaller boats floated in and out of the harbor. Above them, the bridge spanned the bay. *Climb the Harbour Bridge.* That was definitely on the list. Someday.

"What happens when you get an assignment from a company you don't believe in?" he asked.

Jackson sighed. "I try to find something redeeming about them. But someday I'd like to be able to pick and choose my jobs."

"What would you choose?" he asked.

She laughed. "Definitely more international locations. Maybe Paris?"

If this trip went well, maybe she could. Now that she was getting some of the larger clients, there might be more international travel in her future.

"What do you think about Blackmore Inc.?" he asked. "Have you found something redeeming about us yet?"

She laughed. "Are you fishing for compliments?"

Cameron grinned and rubbed the back of his neck. "You have a whole file on me. I'm just trying to figure out what I'm in for these next two weeks."

She raised an eyebrow at him.

They had somehow found themselves walking closer, and his hand brushed against hers. He didn't move away, and neither did she. He fell into step next to her, and for a moment she let herself forget he was Cameron Blackmore. She let him be the man he was last night: funny, smooth-talking and tempting as hell. And this time he was in a little better focus. He was such a physical presence that she'd have trouble ignoring him, even if she didn't know just how good a night with him could be. And now that she knew?

Cameron pointed ahead to where the pedestrian walk split. One path led up to the Sydney Opera House, and another lower path continued along the water. Nestled below the higher path was an outdoor bar with tables.

"There's the place where we're headed," he said.

But as they came closer, his easy smile disappeared. They had managed to bridge the awkwardness of their eye-opening introduction for a little while, but that bridge had disappeared. He widened his paces, and Jackson took a couple quick steps to keep up.

Cameron approached the hostess and grumbled a few indecipherable words at her. The woman nodded and led them inside, underneath the upper level of the promenade, to a table in the back corner of the restaurant. As Jackson's eyes adjusted to the dim light, she recognized the three men sitting around the table from their photos. They were all a lot larger in person.

The blond guy, the one who had been caught whispering in the high-profile actress's ear, took one long look at her and turned to Cameron.

"You brought a date to this meeting, you fuckwit?" he said with a laugh.

Cameron's growl rolled through his chest. "Max Jensen, meet Jackson McAllister. And, yes, he's always this charming."

Max sized her up with new appreciation, and his

smile grew wider. He stood up and stuck out his hand. "Welcome to Sydney, Ms. McAllister. I trust Cameron's made you feel welcome."

There was no good way to answer that comment. She shook his hand and gave him a neutral smile. "Nice to meet you."

The other two stood up.

A dark-haired man with stunning green eyes extended his hand next. "Simon Rodriguez," he said.

The last man stepped forward, the one who was pictured with his wife. This guy was the biggest of the group, probably a Pacific Islander, and he was by far the most relaxed. "Derek Latu," he said, reaching out his hand. She shook it, and they all sat down.

The table was silent. Right. Best to get straight to the point.

"I'm sure you're all thrilled to have me here," she said.

The three men chuckled.

"I didn't come to tell you all what to do," she continued. "The numbers suggest you're doing a great job running this business. But after some recent press, the board wants an image adjustment. I'm here to help with that."

She looked around the table for reactions. They were all looking between her and Cameron. So she hazarded a glance at him, too. He was sitting straight up in his chair, arms crossed, with a rock-hard expression on his face. A flush crept up his neck, and she wondered how a man this easily provoked could make it in the security business. She almost laughed.

"Mr. Blackmore, did you want to add something?" she asked calmly.

He shook his head. Derek smirked.

The waitress appeared, and Jackson let out her breath. The woman set down a round of beers in front of the men. Cameron took a long drink from the bottle, finishing half before he set it down.

"What would you like to drink, ma'am?"

Should she order wine? Nope, probably not a good idea. Jackson was going to need all her wits about her for this meeting, especially if Cameron was already this worked up.

"Just water please," she said.

The waitress left in silence. This was going to be painful. She reached into her bag and pulled out a pad of paper.

"Let's take care of this," she said and turned back to the other three. "I'm here to test a couple key public relations opportunities to see what works best and plan accordingly. So as per the board's instructions, I'll spend a few days tailing Mr. Blackmore. I'll shadow one of your jobs—"

"What?" Cameron snapped.

Jackson raised an eyebrow. "I thought that was clear."

"This isn't a sporting event, Ms. McAllister." His voice held contempt. "It's private security that has the potential to be dangerous for everyone involved. It's not for spectators, no matter what the board says." He rubbed his forehead and muttered, "What the hell are they thinking?"

Cameron had a point. What the hell *was* the board thinking? The Blackmore Inc. team was supposed to do their job and make sure Jackson got a good view? From what she'd heard of this board from her colleagues at the PR firm, this sounded like another one of their armchair decisions that had little to do with reality. It wouldn't be the first. Or maybe this was Harlan Blackmore's more personal directive, aimed to take Cameron down a notch. Perhaps Cameron deserved some sympathy… She might have felt bad for him if he wasn't still sneering in her direction. She met his glare and tipped up her chin at him. "The board is thinking that I can take care of myself just fine, Mr. Blackmore," she said slowly, as if she were explaining this to a child.

Cameron clamped his jaw shut and Jackson fought not to roll her eyes. Enough of Cameron Blackmore's caveman tantrums. She had to get out of here and regain her composure.

"If you'll excuse me," she said and headed for the ladies' room.

CHAPTER FIVE

CAMERON WATCHED JACKSON disappear in silence. Only after the door closed did he breathe a sigh of relief.

He turned back to his team. Each was watching him with varying degrees of amusement on their faces.

"Well, that was interesting," said Simon with a grin. "And informative."

Derek raised his eyebrows. "I'm not convinced you're going to make it through this dinner without exploding, let alone two weeks. But it's a fun show to watch."

They all snickered. Cameron pressed his lips together.

"I don't know why you're so wound up, Cam," said Max. "So she's hot. That should make the next few days much more entertaining. Though I don't get the feeling she's the type to—"

"Shut the hell up, all of you," said Cameron.

All three of them laughed at him. He grumbled a few curses under his breath.

"Come on, Cameron. You gotta admit this is a little funny," said Simon. "We've been in a shitload of intense situations, and you have never once shown signs of cracking. But one day with an attractive woman telling you what to do and you're getting ready to detonate."

"Hilarious," growled Cameron. "It's only my company that's on the line."

That sobered them all up a bit.

He heaved out a long breath. Any time he had gotten involved with someone he'd worked with, he had always waited until the job was over. And it only took one night to scratch that itch before it was gone. So why the hell wasn't this under control?

All afternoon, he had told himself that once the shock of seeing her in the office wore off, everything would return to normal. But she'd ended up in his arms more than once since then. This day was almost over and he was still far from under control.

The last straw was the walk along the harbor. Talking as if they were on some sort of date. As if she and her firm weren't hired by Harlan Blackmore to get Cameron back in line. But as soon as the restaurant came into sight, reality had hit him. She was here because Cameron's successes at Blackmore Inc. were reminders of his father's failures.

He had to get his shit together.

Derek sighed. "I get that you can't stand what the board is doing, but like you said, it's just a couple weeks. You've been in far worse situations. And maybe she can help show the board how important the monitoring side of the business is becoming."

"Maybe you could try to just be decent to her," said Simon. "That might work. Just a thought."

What was he supposed to say? That he had already put their company on the line by screwing the woman that could torpedo their jobs? And now he couldn't stop thinking about what else he wanted to do with her, to her. At least they hadn't gotten into anything dirtier...

"Here she comes," Simon murmured.

Jackson sat down and flipped through her notepad to a bullet-pointed page. She read her first point and began with questions about the team's daily routines. Her voice was clipped and professional, and she didn't once glance in Cameron's direction. He didn't hear a word she said.

Just try to be decent to her? What the hell did *decent* look like when just waiting next to her for the elevator was enough to get him hard? He was supposed to spend the next week alone with her, on full alert, never once slipping up. That alone was bad enough, but struggling through this in front of his team was pushing him over the edge fast.

Even the way Max was looking at her now made his blood boil. And Max wasn't even trying to pick her up. What the hell was wrong with him?

"It's all at your place, isn't it, Cameron?" said Derek.

Cameron blinked. "Sorry. What's at my place?"

"The master list of all clients," said Derek, raising an eyebrow.

Jackson looked at him, all business. "I need it for the conference with the board tomorrow morning."

Cameron shook his head. "It doesn't leave my apartment. That stipulation is written into some of our clients' contracts."

"I need to verify the photos against the client list," she said.

"Not going to happen," said Cameron. "You'll have to trust us when we tell you they're clients."

"That's not going to happen, Mr. Blackmore," Jackson said, matching his tone perfectly. "I'm here because trusting you isn't working for the board."

He bit back an angry retort. The other three were watching this exchange, back and forth, waiting for someone to falter. But Jackson didn't. Her cool gaze was fixed on him, waiting for his next move.

Simon cleared his throat. "As entertaining as this is to watch, I'm going to jump in here with an easy solution. Why doesn't Ms. McAllister go to your place tonight and look at the client list? It never leaves your place, and Ms. McAllister gets to verify the names in person."

Jackson's eyes widened and Cameron froze. Jackson in his apartment? No way.

"Fine. That sounds like a good solution," said Jackson, her voice a little higher.

The whole table turned to him.

"Fine," mumbled Cameron. "Fine." He looked up and met Derek's gaze. His friend glanced at Jackson and back at him, a deep line forming between his eyebrows. Cameron turned away. The last thing he wanted was for Derek to think through this situation further.

Jackson didn't miss a beat. She consulted her bullet-pointed list and asked her next question. But Cameron couldn't move on. Him and Jackson alone in his apartment tonight? Not fine at all.

By the time they left the restaurant, Cameron still hadn't come up with a good reason why Jackson shouldn't go back to his place that night. But the master list never left the privacy of his home. Any other solution had the potential to betray the confidentiality of his most vulnerable—or most secretive—clients. And he wasn't ready to stoop as low as claiming sudden food poisoning to get out of this visit. Almost, but not quite. Besides, excuses would only delay the problem, not solve it.

So, he found himself standing at Circular Quay with Jackson as his private launch arrived to take them home. The captain, Ralph, helped Jackson climb in, and Cameron followed after her. She hadn't looked at him once since they'd left the restaurant. It was going to be a long, hard night in every way possible.

She didn't say a word as they left the dock. Her eyes widened as they passed the Opera House and then she turned for a view of the Harbour Bridge. He leaned back against his seat and watched her. Strands of her lustrous brown hair escaped from the bun and whipped across her face as the boat picked up speed. The corners of her mouth turned up. In the restaurant she was all business, but now, as she looked out into the harbor, she looked softer, the way she'd looked the night before.

The thought dampened his already pessimistic outlook for the evening. He was going to spend the next hour or two trying not to think about all the things he'd rather be doing with her in his apartment.

The launch glided through the waters into his little harbor. Ralph tied up the boat at a private jetty, and he and Jackson wordlessly made their way across the dock to his building. The silence grew heavier as they rode the elevator up to his apartment.

She took the fastener out of her hair to retighten the knot, and he crossed his arms, willing himself not to look at the front of her silky blouse, where one too many buttons had come undone in the process. He was not going to look at the tops of two of the most delicious breasts he had ever seen. Why the hell hadn't he focused more on them the night before? Finally, the elevator doors opened, and Cameron stepped out first. He wasn't going to watch her from behind again. He entered his penthouse, hung his jacket in the hall closet and headed for his bedroom.

"You can wait in there," he said to Jackson, gesturing toward the dining room. "I'll be right back with the list."

When he returned, he found her waiting by the window, looking over the harbor. He sat down at the table and opened his laptop. She spoke to him without turning around.

"Your office isn't your only view of the Harbour Bridge," she murmured. "I like this one even better."

"Thanks." He looked out at the water. He had chosen this penthouse apartment for its view, but how long had it been since he'd actually enjoyed it? All the money spent on furniture and rugs and whatever else the com-

pany's decorator had chosen to fill this place was a
waste. But the board had insisted. A CEO didn't live in
a 300-square-foot apartment without a sofa.

"Head of a successful company in Australia, apart-
ment with a view, commute in your own private boat."
She sighed. "Quite a life you have for yourself, Mr.
Blackmore."

"Please don't call me Mr. Blackmore. Not here, not
after—" He stopped. He shouldn't even mention it. "It's
Cameron. And yes, I've made a good life here. Probably
should start learning to appreciate it more."

"You should," she said softly. "More than one bedroom in New York is a dream, never mind the view."

She slipped into a chair next to his and pulled out the
folder of press clippings. "I'm sorry to do this to you,
but I need to confirm that each person in the photos is
on your list. If it all checks out, I'll report back to the
board tomorrow morning and let them know these are
clients, not…anything else."

Cameron's jaw clenched. What the hell? "So the
board sent you over to make a list of who my team
might have taken home?" growled Cameron. His day
was getting worse by the minute.

"Don't flatter yourself," Jackson said coolly. "No one
cares how much mediocre sex you have. The board just
cares about your company's image. So let's move on."

Cameron's jaw dropped open. *Mediocre sex?* Was
she implying that their night together was mediocre?
No. Impossible. The night before was fantastic. She'd
thought so, too…hadn't she?

Jackson picked up one of the photos from her file.

"Mr. Blackmore?" she asked in a sugary tone. "Can we get on with this?"

He grunted some approximation of yes.

"Good," she said. "How do you want to work this?"

"I can't show you the whole client list. We're very careful with our clients' privacy, even if the board isn't." He narrowed his eyes, ready for a challenge.

She gave him a look of exaggerated patience. "How about you tell me the name of the person in this photo and show me the name in your database."

"Fine."

She shuffled through the photos, one by one, and he clicked on each corresponding name.

His shoulders tightened with every minute he sat next to her. *Mediocre?* Could it be that he had so completely misjudged her reaction to him last night? Because though he'd been with more than his fair share of women, last night stood out. No. There had been a moment that passed between them yesterday, as she'd looked up at him, and he was under the impression her orgasms were more than satisfying. Both of them.

Maybe she was just taunting him. She must be. He had to believe that, if only because he really didn't want to think about the other men who had tasted her and made her come in some way he hadn't.

Cameron had to find out for sure.

Jackson came to the photo of him and the two women coming out of the bar. She hesitated.

"Names?" she asked, her face blank.

He mirrored her expression. "Alya Petrova is a client. Her sister, Natasha, isn't."

She stared at him, as if she were waiting for more information. He didn't say anything. Let her think the worst. It was Max who couldn't stay away from Natasha, not him. But that was Max's problem. And none of Jackson's business.

She bit her lip.

"Did you want more details?" he asked, crossing his arms.

She shook her head and wrote the names on the photo.

Jackson continued through the rest of the papers, but she didn't look nearly as composed as she had when they started. Good. When they got to the end, she closed her folder and stuffed it in her bag. She stood up and ran a hand down her skirt. He rose to face her. She was close enough that she had to tilt her head up to meet his eyes.

"Is that all you need from me tonight, Jackson?" he asked.

He had meant to provoke her, but when her first name slipped out of his mouth, the question sounded much more seductive. A few more strands of hair had fallen from the knot on top of her head, and she tucked them behind her ear. He shouldn't be pushing her like this. He should just let it go. But he couldn't bring himself to back down, not when she looked so uncertain. And so sexy.

She swallowed. "Yes."

"Good," he said. "I wouldn't want to subject you to another mediocre night."

She met his gaze and shrugged. "It's okay. Not everything can live up to expectations."

A low rumble escaped from his mouth. Live up to her expectations? What the hell kind of expectations did she have?

She smiled at his reaction and continued with a sigh. "Guys like you always think you're better than you really are."

He narrowed his eyes. "Guys like me?"

She counted off his descriptors on her long, slender fingers. "Tall and fit, used to getting your way all the time, want every woman to think you—"

Cameron was done with her list. He closed his hand around hers and said, "Right now, I'm not interested in what any other woman thinks. I want to hear what you think. When you got down on all fours, ready for my cock, was that just mediocre? Or do we need to do something more to satisfy you?"

CHAPTER SIX

JACKSON'S HEART POUNDED in her chest, and she bit her lip to keep from smiling. Shit. How the hell had this moved so quickly into dangerous territory? Actually, she knew the answer. She had been aching for a chance to push his buttons the way he'd pushed hers all evening. He wouldn't back down from a challenge. So she'd gone straight for it.

And now he had taken the bait.

She could lie to him and end this stupid game right now. She could tell him that their night wasn't exceptional and she wasn't interested in another. He wouldn't push her. That would be her smartest move right now. Just shut this whole conversation down and leave his annoyingly luxurious apartment. But she couldn't bring herself to do it.

Still, Cameron didn't need yet another ego boost. She couldn't tell him that "satisfied" didn't even begin to capture the glow of their night. He had probably heard gushing praise from the long list of women in his one-night-stand history, and Jackson wasn't interested in getting in that line. Or even thinking about it.

So what the hell did she do now?

She stared at the way his hand fit around hers. Damn, he was big. And he waited her out with an arrogant, impossible-to-ignore stance. The wide muscled wall of his chest was directly in her line of sight. Close enough to touch. She balled her fist, resisting.

Then, slowly, he rubbed a calloused thumb up and down the inside of her palm. He leaned forward until his lips were next to her ear, but he didn't touch her. "You weren't satisfied when I got down on my knees and licked you until you couldn't stand?"

Jackson let out a little moan. Shit. She was in so much trouble right now. Her fingers trembled. How much longer could she keep herself together?

"What's your answer?" he whispered. "You can't blame it on bad eyesight this time."

He was going to keep taunting her until she called his bluff.

She couldn't help herself.

She took off her glasses and dropped them in her bag. Then she wove her fingers into his hair. She found his lips with hers and pressed a slow, hungry kiss on them. He groaned and opened his mouth to hers. When her tongue touched his, it was as if his whole body lit up. He let go of her other hand and one big arm came around her back while the other slipped under her rear and pulled her against him. His enormous erection grew against her thigh, and she smiled. Right now, he wanted her just as badly as she wanted him. And that was probably as close to a win as she was going to get tonight.

She sucked his bottom lip between hers and gently bit down. His big body tensed and thrust against her. He pulled away, panting, and met her eyes.

"Done refreshing your memory?" he breathed, the corners of his mouth turning up.

Damn. She should have known he wasn't going to let go of this topic so easily. Still, she wasn't going to tell him what he wanted to hear: that he was amazing in bed. Even if he was. Jackson searched for another diversion.

"This isn't a good idea."

He chuckled. "What the hell is the difference between doing this once or twice?"

Well, he had a point.

Cameron pressed his hips against hers, and her breath caught. One hand found her breast. "It's just a question of whether or not you think you'll be…satisfied."

As the last word came out of his mouth, he pinched her hard nipple through her shirt. She cried out. How could he get her body going so easily? All she wanted was for him to do it again and again.

He closed his eyes, seeming to savor her reaction, and his erection pressed harder against her. She squirmed against his big body, seeking more contact. For a moment, he looked like he was struggling to hold himself together just as much as she was. But when he spoke again, his voice betrayed no weakness.

"Did you wake up thinking about me this morning? Wanting me inside you?"

He was *not* going to push her into lying. But, damn, he was already so full of himself.

"Maybe," she tried. It came out more as a whimper than a challenge.

Cameron's face lit up into a wide smile, and he started to laugh, a deep, low laugh of amusement. "Now we're getting somewhere."

Jackson couldn't hold back much longer. Her own laughter grew inside until she leaned her head forward on his chest and let it out. He let go of her breast and wrapped his arm around her shoulders, pulling her closer. Breathing him in, she relaxed a little. It felt way too good to be there.

She tilted her head, and when she met his deep blue eyes again, the cool distance in his expression was gone.

"What do you think, Ms. Jackson McAllister?" he rumbled. "This has been one hell of a ride today. How do you want it to end?"

She blinked. After their long day of sparring, he was giving in. His guard was down, and behind it there was a hint of tenderness. This was the man she'd caught a glimpse of at the end of last night; the man who had covered her with a blanket and looked at her so seriously, so quietly before he left.

His defenses would come back up soon. Considering his reputation, there was a chance that this side of him wasn't even real. But right now, it felt real.

Sex with someone like him wouldn't—couldn't—be tender, but that wasn't what she wanted.

"I've wanted you all day long," she admitted.

His body tightened against hers, and he drew in a sharp breath. Damn, he was tempting. She wanted to see him react to her again. All her dirty thoughts from the day came at once, and she started with the first.

"When I caught you looking down my shirt this morning, I had this fantasy. I wanted to kneel down between your legs," she whispered, her voice husky. "I wanted to suck you off right there in your office. And make you desperate the way you made me desperate last night. I wanted to hear you beg to come in my mouth. And I'd let you."

"Fuuuck." He shuddered.

His hips flexed against hers. He was thick and hard and hit on all the right places. She had never talked like this before to a man, but if they were going for it tonight, she might as well let it all loose. They had already stepped over the line. And she had a thousand ideas about where to take it.

"You wanna make that fantasy come true right now?"

"Yes," she whispered.

He let her go, and for a moment, she thought he was going to call it all off. That this had been just another game to jockey for power.

But he grabbed her hand and led her to the living room. A man this sexy didn't deserve to have a sitting room this nice, too. Sparse but warm. Black leather couch, white shag rug and art Cameron Blackmore couldn't have picked for himself. Or maybe he did. She really knew almost nothing personal about this man.

Aside from what it was like to have his mouth between her legs.

Cameron leaned against the back of his sofa, and gave her a dark smile.

She toyed with the buttons on her blouse. "If you want something, you need to ask for it," she whispered.

He reached down and stroked himself. "I want you to take me out and suck me. Deep."

Jackson closed her eyes at the erotic rush radiating through her. If last night was sexy as hell, this was even more intense. He was giving a bit of control over to her. Where would that take them?

He pulled his shirt over his head to reveal the insanely carved muscles of his chest. A jagged scar cut across his ribs—she hadn't noticed it the night before. She knelt down in front of him and unbuttoned his pants. His erection pressed against them as she eased down his zipper. It opened up to his boxers, where a wet circle covered his tip.

"Take it out," he rasped.

She eased his boxers over his hips, revealing his thick, hard length. Oh, God. She had seen him last night, but up close his size was still overwhelming.

Cameron leaned against the back of the sofa and spread his legs.

She stepped back and continued to unbutton her shirt, slowly, drawing out each movement. He brought his hand down to his erection for a few final hard tugs, his gaze fixed on her chest. "Just thinking about your breasts all day made me hard."

She let her blouse fall to the floor.

"You're beautiful," he whispered. He rested his hand on the sofa and smiled. "You can taste and play all you want. But I like it rough when I finish. Is that okay with you?"

His eyes were dark and half-closed...with lust?

"I want you to show me just how rough you like it," she said.

He squeezed his eyes shut, as she moved closer, and his erection bobbed enthusiastically.

Jackson reached for his rock-hard length and her body tingled with all sorts of ideas for how this could go. Would he grab her hair? Would he show her how to take more? What did he like best? She tried a few experimental swipes of her tongue. God, he tasted like dirty sex, so she licked him again. She ran her tongue down his long length and up again. He took a sharp breath, so she ran her tongue down it again, stopping at his base.

"Suck on my balls," he groaned.

She took one in her mouth and played with it, then the other. He muttered a low string of incomprehensible words.

She replaced her mouth with her hand and caressed a little more.

Her gaze darted up to his. He was staring at her, watching everything she did with a dark intensity in his eyes. He was unbelievably gorgeous.

"What else do you want?" A tremor ran through his body as she spoke.

"Suck me hard, Jackson," he said through clenched teeth. "I want to give you a mouthful."

She smiled. This was what she wanted. To make him unravel before her, from the power of her touch. God, this was hot. Her own body was on fire as she leaned forward and put her lips around him. He moaned, and she took him deeper. Playing with different techniques, she drew out and in.

His hands wove into her hair, tugging at her fastener, and her waves tumbled down her back. He grabbed on and guided her in and out, setting the pace. His breaths were short and harsh. His hips lifted off the edge of the sofa as he began to thrust into the back of her mouth. Deeper. She gagged, and he froze.

"Shit," he snarled. "Sorry, sweetheart."

She pulled back and looked at him. "I don't want you to be gentle," she whispered. "I want exactly what you're giving me. I want you to lose control."

Her own voice was breathy and full of need. His grip on her hair tightened, and she took him back into her mouth. She reached between her own legs and teased herself. Whoa. She was getting close, too. She sucked hard, and with a groan he took over. Having him in her mouth was perversely erotic. She angled his erection down her throat until he lost his rhythm. He flexed hard and came with a loud growl. Jackson's body was alive with raw, crude pleasure as he panted and shuddered above her.

He unclenched her hair and bent over her, muttering curses. She released him, and he smoothed her hair down her back in soft, almost reverent strokes. He kissed the top of her head, then tucked himself in and held out a hand to help her up.

Jackson's knees ached, and she was a little dizzy from the whole experience.

"I think I should sit down," she said.

He rubbed his eyes and nodded. He still hadn't said anything, and she wasn't sure what she wanted to say, either.

Jackson picked up her blouse and walked to the other side of the dark sofa. She sank into the soft pillows and took a couple long breaths. What now? Did she just grab her bag and leave?

Cameron rustled behind her. His arms wrapped around her from the back of the sofa, and he bent down so his breath was in her ear.

"That was so good," he said, his voice rough.

She nodded.

"Unbelievably good."

Jackson smiled. "For me, too." She turned to look at him, and the corners of his mouth kicked up.

He let go of her, and cool air brushed over her skin. He came around the sofa and knelt down in front of her, resting his hands on her thighs.

"We're not done here," he said.

Why wasn't this a good idea? She could barely remember at this point. Besides, this might be her last chance with Cameron. She swallowed and whispered, "Okay."

"Okay?" Cameron laughed. "You're going to have to do better than that, sweetheart."

He angled a pillow on the arm of the sofa and nodded for her to turn and lean back on it. He guided one of her legs up to rest on the back of the couch and scooted her skirt up over her hips.

"Now, let's try that again," he said, climbing onto the couch between her open legs. He rested back on his heels and smiled. "Do you want me to get you off?" There was dark heat in his eyes, and he put a hand down his boxers and adjusted himself.

She could ask for anything she wanted right now, and he would do it. Should she ask for something that guaranteed pleasure, or was this the once-in-a-lifetime chance to try something that she never thought she would. His question from the night before came back to her. *Have you ever played here?* If anyone could do that right, it was certainly Cameron Blackmore. Her pulse thumped in her throat.

No. Some things were probably better left to the imagination.

Jackson licked her lips as she made her decision. "I want you to get me off with your mouth," she said.

Cameron smiled with a look of smug satisfaction. "You can watch me."

He lowered himself between her legs and started slowly, teasing her thighs and kissing her through her panties. When she moved to slip off the piece of silk, Cameron laughed, tickling her.

"Be patient. I want to take my time with this."

And he did. He explored the inside of her legs, around each sensitive spot. He was leisurely and thorough, and the deep groans mingling with her breathy sighs told her that he was enjoying it as much as she was. As she lifted her hips and arched with pleasure toward his mouth, he held her tighter, attending to each different place, testing her responsiveness. He was relentless, building her up and then easing her down, over and over until she grabbed his hair.

"Please, Cameron," she panted. "Now."

He swirled his tongue, focusing on her clit, pushing her over the edge as she bucked her hips against him. Everything exploded in white-hot shards of pleasure through her. He didn't stop. He drew out her orgasm until it subsided in gentle waves. She let go of his hair, and he sat back. He was a beautiful sight, all tense muscles and a look of triumph on his face. She was open and exposed, but she didn't move. She just watched him. He wiped his mouth with the back of his hand and smiled.

Then he met her eyes, and slowly he lowered his body over hers. His erection throbbed urgently against her, but the rest of him was under tight control. He kissed her on the lips and gave her a soft bite on the neck.

"I want to be inside you so bad, Jackson," he whispered in her ear. "And I don't know if I'll ever get a chance to do it again."

"So do it now," she said.

He rolled his hips into hers with a deep groan. One of his hands cupped her face, and he kissed her.

"It's going to be fast and hard," he said, his lips brushing against hers.

"I like fast and hard," she said.

"Good." He eased back and pulled the wallet out of his back pocket to grab a condom. He lowered his boxers. Did his girlfriends ever get used to his sex drive? But he'd said himself he wasn't the type that had girlfriends.

Cameron tore off the wrapper and rolled the condom down his impressive length. He lifted one of her legs to rest on his shoulder, and he teased her, gliding over her firmly.

"You want this?" he growled.

"Yes," she breathed.

He positioned himself and then slammed into her. Oh, God. She cried out at the overwhelming fullness, and Cameron's face twisted in agonizing pleasure. He pulled out and started to move. He swore and thrust harder. All of his tight control dissolved. It was as if he had given in and let something deeper, something more basic, take over. His eyes were dark and alive, and her body sang under his. Her hips matched his rhythmic movements, seeking a second release that finally came. Explosive pleasure washed over her. He drove into her a few more times and threw his head back in an enormous roar. His big body jerked as he came.

He fell down onto his arms, his head hanging over her. He closed his eyes, and his chest heaved. She wanted to pull him down and feel the weight of him on her. She wanted to draw out the deep satisfaction of this encounter.

But that wasn't what this night was about. That wasn't what Cameron Blackmore was about.

She shifted under him, and he blinked his eyes open. He looked down at her. His gaze was soft, full of wonder. He opened his mouth as if to speak, but he seemed to change his mind. Instead he pulled out and took off his condom.

"You are really fucking hot," he said as he got off the couch and headed for the kitchen.

That was what he wanted to say to her? That she was hot? That look on his face had moved her. Damn him. He had to go and spoil this night by opening his stupid mouth. Because for a moment, she'd almost gotten carried away. For a moment, she'd thought they had hit on something more.

But all things considered, this was probably the best way to end the night. Call it a reality check.

Quickly she squirmed off the couch and shimmied her crushed skirt back over her hips. She shuffled the pillows and dug up her shirt, now crumpled into an ugly mess. She shoved her arms into the sleeves and buttoned it up.

Cameron wandered back into the room with two glasses of water in his hands, but he stopped when he caught sight of her.

"Jackson?" he said. "Are you leaving?"

She had to get out of his apartment before she did anything stupid. He hadn't deceived her. She knew this encounter wasn't about anything more than pleasure, and he had just taken her orgasm to a new level. So why the hell did she feel like snapping at him?

Jackson put on her best business face and smiled. "Early calls, meeting tomorrow with the board. As you know."

She found her way to his ridiculously stylish dining room table and picked up her bag, but by the time she reached the elevator door, Cameron was standing in front of it.

"What's going on, Jackson?" he asked.

"Absolutely nothing is going on, Cameron," she said smoothly, forcing another smile. "Isn't that the point of this?"

She stared at him, challenging him to disagree. He didn't. His deep blue eyes were guarded, wary as he looked down at her. The elevator door opened.

"Excuse me," she said, motioning to the door.

He stepped aside and she walked in. The doors closed, and she shoved her hand into her bag, searching for her glasses. It was only when she reached the street that Jackson realized she had no idea how to get back to her hotel room.

CHAPTER SEVEN

CAMERON BLACKMORE YANKED open the door to his office building. More accurately, his father's office building. It was one of many assets that Cameron had added to the Blackmore Inc. empire, all ultimately controlled by his father.

Cameron was a thorn in his father's side that would never go away. If he had been a little older, a little more experienced when his grandfather died, Harlan Senior would have bypassed Cameron's father altogether and named him chairman of the board. Cameron knew it. His father knew it. The board knew it.

But what Harlan Junior couldn't understand was that Cameron had no desire to take over his job. He'd much rather be in the Sydney office with his team than in a boardroom in New York. Which meant he never had to see another airplane in his life. Let one of his half brothers take on that role and leave Cameron as the master of his own domain.

Harlan Blackmore was good at bullshit like country clubs and photo ops—much better at schmoozing than he was at the actual business of running a company.

But no matter what his father threw his way, Cameron wouldn't walk away from his grandfather's legacy. His father had used Cameron's strong sense of loyalty to keep him in line in the aftermath of his parents' awful divorce. And now he was counting on this same sense of loyalty to Harlan Senior to keep Cameron from rebelling against the board outright.

Which was the reason Cameron was in this current mess in the first place.

Though there was no way to blame last night's mess on his father. That fell squarely on his own shoulders. He had replayed the scene at least a hundred times since the elevator doors closed behind her, and he still couldn't shake the hurt on Jackson's face.

Telling her she was hot was about the stupidest thing he had done in a while, and considering the last two days of stupid moves, that was saying something. He had thrown it out to cover up what almost came out of his mouth as he looked down at Jackson, still buried deep inside of her. He'd almost told her that he wanted to do this every day for the rest of his life. That this was what he had been missing. And that would have taken this messed-up situation to a new level of messed-up-ness.

Cameron walked into the elevator and punched the button for the top floor. He gritted his teeth. His entire business depended on his ability to plan, to foresee all potential problems, to make everything run smoothly, but nothing about the last two days had gone right. And he had only a couple hours to come up with a new plan to dig himself out of the latest hole he'd made.

Then Jackson McAllister would show up at the office again.

"Good morning, Mr. Blackmore," Chloe chirped as he walked through the glass doors. "Mr. Latu, Mr. Jensen and Mr. Rodriguez are waiting for you in the large conference room."

Right. First he had to get through this meeting. These guys knew him better than anyone else in the world. One of them was going to figure out how badly he had screwed up soon. Judging from the night before at dinner, Cameron had his money on Derek. But that wasn't going to happen today. Soon this meeting would be over and he'd have time to do a little thinking in the weight room before he had to face Jackson again.

And figure out how not to botch this situation further.

He grabbed the handle to the conference room door and took a deep breath. Game time. He swung it open.

Derek, Max and Simon sat around one end of the long table. Max was in the middle of a story, and the other two sat back in the black leather chairs, watching.

"After we're done I say—" Max turned toward him and smiled. "Cam, just in time."

Derek punched Max on the shoulder. "No way that story ends with 'Cam, just in time.'"

Simon and Max chuckled.

"I'll finish it later," said Max. "Where's your baby-sitter, mate?"

Cameron sat down in one of the chairs and let out a long breath. "She's got a video conference with the board. She'll be here in a couple of hours."

They all watched him silently, no doubt waiting for more details. Cameron didn't say a word.

Finally Derek broke the silence. "I'm just going to lay it all out for us. We need a new plan. I'm not feeling the idea of undermining Jackson McAllister's reputation. Plus, I'm pretty sure we'd come off as sexist."

Max leaned back in his chair and smiled. "How's this for a new plan? One of us takes her out and gets caught with her in some sort of compromising situation. I doubt the board sends anyone here after that. And she's gorgeous, so I'll volunteer myself for the job. A woman like that's all business on the outside, but when you get her—"

"No!" barked Cameron. He heaved in a calming breath, but the damage was done. Already he was picturing Max and Jackson together. Jackson moaning and calling out Max's name instead of his. Cameron ground his teeth together hard.

No. Just no.

Cameron unclenched his fists. "No one messes with her," he bit out. "Don't bring it up again. Our plan isn't going to work."

Max rolled his eyes. "Okay, boss."

Derek crossed his arms and sighed. "Hate to mention this, Cam, but how about just finding a way through that flying problem of yours and taking it up with your father and the board in person?"

Cameron shook his head. "Not an option."

They had been over this before. The doctors had called it PTSD, but who the hell would be crazy enough to get on a plane after a crash like his unit had been through?

Derek threw up his hands. "Help me out here, Simon. You talk to him."

Simon shook his head. "Not helping on this one, Derek. Staying away from airplanes is Cameron's thing. Other guys in our unit came home with much more fucked up ways of dealing with it. If he says no, I'm letting it be."

Cameron shot Simon a nod of thanks. They'd been through hell together, and Cam knew his friend had his own reasons for not returning to the States—airplanes had nothing to do with it. "We're just going to get through this. We let her babysit for two weeks, and then it's done."

Max raised an eyebrow, but Cameron ignored him.

"We're moving on," he said. "Ms. McAllister had a bunch of photos that looked like all of us cozying up with clients. Most were on the job, but a few weren't. The press doesn't always get it right. Sometimes they catch us during off hours, but we need to watch that. Not just while she's here. In the future, too."

He looked at Simon and Max. They nodded.

"But there was one photo you all need to see." Cameron pulled the sheet from his briefcase and set it on the table.

Derek grabbed it. "What the fuck?" he said.

"I know," said Cameron. "Take it easy."

Max leaned over to get a look at the paper crushed in Derek's hand. "Is that Laurie?"

"It is," said Cameron. "I checked out the address on the top of the papers. It comes from a social media account, last name Toleafoa. Samoan, right, Derek?"

Derek's jaw clenched tightly, and his lips formed a tight snarl. He gave a curt nod.

"It's Derek's name on the caption, not Laurie's. Scrolling through this guy's other posts, I'm pretty sure his only interest in Laurie is that she's with Derek, not the other way around."

Derek closed his eyes and leaned back in his chair. "I won't let her go through that again," he said softly.

"None of us will, Derek," said Simon, clapping his friend on the shoulder.

Cameron nodded. "Right. And you know I wouldn't play down the risk if I thought there was one."

Derek opened his eyes and met Cameron's. The hard look softened a little. "Okay. But I still think this is messed up. Even if this guy didn't recognize Laurie, someone else could."

"Exactly," said Cameron. "This is why I brought the photo this morning. My father and his board sent Ms. McAllister here to adjust our image, but here is the real reason we need to take this PR thing seriously." He gestured to the photo. "More media interest in what we do, including on our off hours, means more photos like this. Or worse. And we can't have that. Our clients require absolute discretion for their safety."

For once, Max looked serious. He glanced at Derek and then turned back to Cameron. "You're right," he said quietly.

Simon nodded. "And not just this week."

"Right," said Cameron.

He leaned back in his chair and let the others digest the information. Derek picked up the photo again and studied it. He looked at Cameron.

"Do I want to take this home and look it up?"

Cameron frowned. "I'm pretty sure you don't."

Derek nodded. "I thought so."

"One of us will watch it for you," said Simon.

Derek took one last look at the photo and passed it back to Cameron. "Okay. Let's move on."

Jackson spent the morning in her hotel room, on a video conference call with the board. Then she set to rereading Blackmore Inc.'s annual report. She had read it on the plane ride over, but now that she had met Cameron Blackmore, her original plans weren't going to work.

She had assumed he was just another self-centered asshole with an overinflated sense of entitlement. She hadn't necessarily revised the self-centered asshole part, but he was a lot more serious about his business than she had expected. Ignoring the board's push for a more prestigious image felt like a *screw you* to Harlan Blackmore rather than a lack of self-control among the men. In fact, the more she studied the company's information, the more she was convinced of just how careful and calculating Cameron was.

Which made her all the angrier about his comment the night before. He must have sensed her momentary lapse in judgment when he rested over her, still inside of her. The whole encounter had been beyond amazing, but when he looked down at her with what had looked like awe, she had almost taken his face in both her hands and told him exactly what she was thinking. That he wasn't at all what she'd expected. That he made her feel better than anyone ever had.

Thank God she hadn't. She had completely misread him. Of course. A careful and calculating man known for his appearances with some high-profile women knew how to cultivate that feeling of intimacy they'd shared. She didn't assume the media had all the facts straight about his affairs, but she also didn't doubt for a second that Cameron Blackmore had his fair share of lovers. He clearly knew what women wanted. But that didn't make any of it real. His comment last night was a message: game over. And she got that message loud and clear. The fact that it hurt told her that she should never repeat a night like that with him, even if they weren't in danger of getting caught.

Cameron hadn't misled her. He had been perfectly clear the first night in the hotel. He was giving her exactly what he promised: orgasms with his big, hard cock. And yes, he definitely knew how to use it.

She was the one who couldn't just let it be.

She needed to refocus. She was supposed to be revising the PR plan. Most of the tactics she had proposed still worked, but the media coverage ideas were off.

Her phone rang, and her assistant's name popped up on the screen.

"Kyle," she said. "How's the northern half of the world today?"

"Cold. And busy." His voice was as chipper as ever. Jackson glanced at her laptop clock, still set to New York time. It was 6:30 p.m.—yesterday?—and the man sounded like he was just starting his day. Probably the type that only needed six hours of sleep at night. Which was good for her, since he had taken on a chunk of her clients while she was in Sydney.

"What do you have for me?" she asked.

"I'm sending over the finals that art just passed on for three December campaigns. I just wanted to run them by you before I okayed them."

She clicked on the images in Kyle's email, and scanned them. "Nice. The second one should probably be a shade or two lighter so that everything still shows up on a smaller scale, but otherwise they're good to go."

"Right, lighter," said Kyle. "I should have seen that."

Jackson laughed. "Don't sweat it. You're the best assistant I've ever had. Give it a little more time and you'll be taking over my job."

"And be assigned to hot Australian clients?" Kyle was definitely smirking now. "That alone is reason enough to work for it. Is he as good-looking in person as he is on paper?"

Thank God this wasn't a video conference because Jackson's face had to be beet red by now.

"He's technically American," she managed to mutter.

"Is that a yes?" Kyle laughed. "I'd take him anyway, though I suspect I'm not his type. But you never know."

Jackson knew exactly what type Cameron was. She flashed to the night before, his naked, muscular torso over her as he came. Shit. She cleared her throat. "I've got to go. Send me the revision of the second file when you get it."

She hung up the phone. *Focus on the job, girl.*

Jackson scanned the company's financial statements. Some of the clients were clear, but others were masked by blandly named corporations. Nothing she could use.

She sighed and looked through the document again. The easiest media coverage to get would be to make a public appearance with a charitable organization, but Blackmore Inc. in Australia didn't seem to give exceptional sums to any one place. Maybe she could convince Cameron to. He could give enough to be newsworthy, she'd send out a press release and they could all deliver the check in person in the next day or two. Perfect.

Jackson closed her laptop and headed for the Blackmore Inc. building.

Twenty minutes later, she stepped out of the elevator into the bright penthouse office.

"Good afternoon, Ms. McAllister," said the receptionist. Chloe, Jackson remembered. She was young and blonde with long, manicured nails and... Jackson frowned. Did Cameron sleep with his receptionist?

"I'm meeting Mr. Blackmore," said Jackson.

The younger woman nodded. "He and Mr. Latu just

headed down to the fifth-floor gym. He said you could set up in the conference room while you wait."

"While I wait?" Jackson echoed.

"They're usually gone for an hour or so."

Jackson huffed out a breath. Wait for Cameron to lift weights and hang out with his friends? Nope.

"Did he take his phone?" she asked.

Chloe shook her head. "He doesn't usually, but you're welcome to try him."

Jackson grimaced and looked at the clock. Okay, so maybe she should have checked in with Cameron this morning if she wanted him to be available. But the thought of calling him? She pinched the bridge of her nose. *Concentrate.*

She needed to get her plan under way: get Cameron to agree to the idea, choose an appropriate charity, arrange for an opportunity to meet the head of the organization and then spread the press release. And she was already getting a late start.

"You said he just went down?" she asked.

"Yes," Chloe said. "I suppose you could catch him coming out of the changing room, but he might be... Never mind."

"I'll find him," said Jackson as she turned back toward the elevators.

The doors opened onto the fifth floor, and Jackson stepped out into a spa-like atrium, with white walls and pictures of water and sand. The hallway in both directions was wide and empty, and the reception desk was unmanned. How did she find her way to the workout room? Listen for sounds of male grunting? She started down the bright hallway, passing doors with unhelpful labels like Room 1 and Room 2. Maybe this wasn't such a good idea.

A door clicked farther down, and low male voices sounded through the hallway. Jackson looked up in time to see a glimpse of ripped ab muscles and a jagged scar before they were covered in a T-shirt. She didn't even have to look up to see who they belonged to. Heat flooded through her, cutting off all rational thought.

"… Afraid I've fucked it all up—" Cameron stopped midsentence as his head came through the neck of his shirt.

"You still have time to fix it—" Derek Latu followed Cameron through the door and came to a stop. He looked at Jackson, at Cameron and back at Jackson again. "Ms. McAllister. This is…unexpected." Derek's face betrayed only mild surprise, but Jackson could tell he was taking her in with new eyes.

"I'll catch you later, bro," he said and headed down the hall.

Jackson waited for the sound of the door closing behind Derek before she let out her breath. "Were you ladies gossiping about your exploits?" she hissed.

Cameron blinked. "No," he said flatly.

"You didn't tell him about…" She waved her hand between them, searching for a good ending to this sentence. Nothing came.

Cameron gave a bark of laughter. "Hell, no."

"Then why was he looking at me like that?"

The corners of Cameron's mouth turned up. "Um. Well, you were staring at me, and you looked…" His eyes danced with amusement. "Let's just say you might have tipped him off."

Jackson leaned back against the wall. She closed her eyes as heat crept up her neck and into her cheeks. Shit. "Really?" she whispered.

"Mmm, really."

His voice was closer, and when she opened her eyes he was standing right in front of her. Not business distance. He was approaching lean-down-and-kiss-the-hell-out-of-her distance.

"No glasses today," he murmured. "Gonna pretend you didn't recognize me again?"

She put up her hand. "Stop right there."

Cameron furrowed his brow.

"I've been known to do really stupid things when you get that close," she said. "I can feel my IQ dropping as we speak."

Cameron stayed put, smiling down at her. "Can I say something?"

She rolled her eyes at him. "Like I could stop you."

"Look, I messed up last night," he said softly. "I was a little thrown off by how things went, and—"

"No." She shook her head to stop this exchange before it got worse. "It's over."

Cameron frowned.

"I know I said the same thing yesterday, but this time I really mean it," she added quickly. "We'll just get through the next two weeks, and when I leave this goes, too."

Cameron shook his head. "It won't be gone."

Jackson put a hand on her hip and raised her eyebrows. "How do you know? How many times have you done this before?"

"Enough to know that it doesn't usually feel like this." He paused. When she didn't say anything, he continued. "Look, it's good between us, really good, and whether or not we act on it doesn't reverse that. I'm already an ass for not keeping my pants on when I told my team to. If you want me to stay away, I will. Probably better that way, but I wouldn't say no if you change your mind. There's a lot we haven't even explored."

His words echoed in erotic waves through her body. Jackson gritted her teeth. How had they got to this point so quickly? "Can we please move on?"

Cameron inhaled slowly and nodded. Jackson straightened up.

"I came down here because I wanted to run something by you," she said, "something I'd like to work on for the rest of the afternoon."

Cameron folded his arms. "I'm listening."

Jackson set down her briefcase and pulled out a folder. "Your charitable donations aren't standout," she said, pointing to the summary she had put together.

The corners of Cameron's mouth turned down. "Is that so?"

Jackson nodded. "I'm thinking you can pick one of the smaller charities the company already gives to, one where you could make a serious difference in their budget, and make a large public donation."

Cameron scowled. "Not that it's any of your business, Ms. McAllister, but I do give. Maybe I should give more, and we can discuss that, but you don't know what the hell you're talking about." He glanced down the hallway and continued. "Second of all, I'm not picking my charities by how much of a PR boost I'll get. I'm not my father. If I'm giving more it's going to UNHCR."

"What's that?" she asked.

"It's the United Nations' fund for refugees."

The acronym hadn't stood out when she looked over the company's financial records earlier. Jackson scanned the papers she was clutching until she found it. "UNHCR...five thousand dollars. For a company of this size, that's not a lot."

He shook his head. "I give a lot more than that."

"Where?" She leafed through the pages. "I don't see anything else."

She looked up at him. He worked his jaw, and his scowl deepened. "Personally. But I'm not using that to boost the company's image."

Cameron stood over her with his arms crossed. She had somehow hit on a nerve, and his defenses were up. She needed to find a way past them. "So, you donate larger sums from your personal finances?" she asked.

He nodded. "Anonymously. But the director knows me. I checked out the organization pretty thoroughly to make sure the money was really being used to help people."

"Why?" she asked. "Why anonymously? Why not as you or under the Blackmore Inc. name?"

The hallway was still and silent, but he glanced up and down again. Then Cameron fixed his gaze on her. "It's my father's name and my father's company now, and he'd twist it for his own advantage. But he doesn't know the first thing about war or refugees or any of the other fallout."

She met his eyes. "And you do."

"Yes," he said quietly. "And I do." He scrubbed a hand over his face. "I don't want to donate money to get the Blackmore name on some flashy building. I've seen some awful things, and there are smart, good people at the UNHCR who know how to help."

"You've been to their office before?"

Cameron nodded. "And I've met some of the people from the refugee camps who relocated to Sydney."

"I see," she murmured. She let the image of Cameron sitting down with refugees sink in. "That must have been intense."

"I guess," he said slowly. "But it's the reality for a lot of people."

Wow. This wasn't where she'd expected this conversation to go. What could she say to that? Jackson had no experience with anything close to war or refugee camps.

"Look, I believed that I was fighting for a good cause when I was on the ground. I still do. But war means terrible things for everyone it touches. I can't ignore that. I have to do something about that part, too."

Oh. She had gotten one thing right the other night. She really didn't know this man.

"I'm impressed, Cameron," she whispered.

He shook his head. "Don't be. I'm going for decent."

She smiled at that, and he studied her for a moment. She wanted to wrap her arms around him and take away the lost look in his eyes. But she couldn't touch him like that. Never again.

Jackson took a deep breath. "I'm not going to push you into this. I can come up with something else. But I just want to add one more thing to consider."

He nodded. "Okay."

"Making a high-profile donation helps the organization, too. They're in the spotlight, and they can leverage the position to raise more money."

Cameron didn't react, but he didn't stop her, so she continued. "Blackmore Inc. will get press for it. Your father might even take the credit. But if that brings in a few thousand dollars to people who really need it, the whole thing might be worth it."

Cameron's face betrayed nothing, but his arms were still crossed tight against his chest.

"Just think about it," she said.

His expression softened. "I will."

CHAPTER EIGHT

"Remind me of why the hell we're on our way to the UNHCR office?" said Derek, smiling across the taxi at Cameron. "I thought you didn't want Blackmore Inc. anywhere near this subject."

Cameron folded his arms. "I changed my mind."

Derek raised an eyebrow. "You changed your mind, or someone changed it for you?"

Cameron groaned. He and Derek had been friends long enough for Cameron to know Derek would keep pushing the subject until he got his answer. And Cameron really didn't want to get into this. At all.

"The board wants some sort of PR boost, and this is a good option," tried Cameron.

"You sure that's it?" asked Derek, his smile growing. "Because when that Ms. Jackson McAllister caught you with your shirt off, she liked what she saw. And I suspect the feeling is mutual."

"Shut the hell up, Derek," he mumbled. "She's the board's PR woman, and she's flying back to New York next week to report on us. It doesn't matter what she liked because nothing's going on. End of story."

Technically, this was true. Nothing was going on because Jackson had put an end to it. Again. But it wasn't anywhere near over in his mind.

Derek chuckled. "You're getting your knickers in a knot over this woman, mate."

Cameron huffed out a breath and looked out the window. "Knickers in a knot" didn't even begin to describe the mess of feelings that were clogging up his thoughts. It wasn't just the flashes of her tousled on his sofa, skirt around her hips, that were tripping him up now. He had mentioned the army. He never talked about that. And when she'd looked at him like she really heard what he was saying, he'd wanted to tell her more. The decision to follow in his grandfather's footsteps, not his father's. The way his father had turned against him. The kind of shit she needed to know if she was going to understand why he never wanted to be in the same room with his father again. That, long before Harlan started meddling with Cameron's job in Sydney, he'd betrayed his son by leaving Cameron and his mother to start a new family.

"Look, something's up." Derek's voice turned more serious. "I don't even want to know what it is. And I'm the last person to tell you to lay off, after what happened with me and Laurie. But be careful. There's a lot riding on this 'PR boost' or whatever the hell they're calling it. For you more than anyone else."

"Don't I know it," said Cameron. He closed his eyes and rubbed his forehead. "What I want is for my father to leave me the hell alone."

Derek was quiet.

"All three of us would understand if you wanted to leave Blackmore Inc.," he finally said.

Cameron frowned. "It's my grandfather's company, not my father's. Harlan Senior was more a father to me, and I owe it to him to stick it out." He clapped Derek's shoulder. "Besides, you three aren't the only salaries the company pays. If I stepped down, my father would fuck up everything I've done."

"You can't keep your father from screwing up other people's lives, Cam." Derek shook his head. "Just take a shot and hope you get it right. I'm sure you will."

"I don't know about that," he muttered.

And Cameron wouldn't rest until he got out from under his father's control. But wasn't that exactly the way Harlan Blackmore thought? Wasn't that why he'd left all those years ago and moved on to his next family—because his father wasn't willing to bend to anyone, not even his own father?

The taxi pulled up in front of the UNHCR offices, and Cameron and Derek climbed out. They stood next to each other on the sidewalk, the traffic at their backs. A PR visit was the last thing in the world Cameron wanted to do right now. Well, almost the last.

Derek cleared his throat. "I wasn't just giving you shit about the thing between Jackson and you. Neither of you are doing a good job of hiding whatever *nothing* is. I don't know what the hell you're doing."

Cameron shook his head. "I don't know what the hell I'm doing, either."

"That's what I thought," Derek said, swinging the door open. "Come on, everyone's up there waiting for us."

By the time they wrapped up at UNHCR, two hours had passed. Cameron led the way out. He pushed open the front door of the building and stepped out onto the sidewalk. The rush of warm city air hit him, and he took a deep breath.

"That was a good move today, Ms. McAllister," said Max from behind him. "Cam, the board will love those pictures with you and the UNHCR directors."

Cameron grunted but didn't turn around.

"It went well." Jackson's voice rang softly in his ears. What the hell was wrong with him? It was like he grew some sort of super-senses when she was around. He couldn't tune anything about her out. They had come into some sort of rhythm the last few days, and her tone shifted when no one else was around. He wanted the time to just watch her, enjoy her. And he didn't have it.

The group stopped next to the street, and Derek looked down at his watch. "I'm headed to the gym," he said. "Anyone else in?"

"I'm in," said Simon.

Max turned to Jackson and flashed her a smile. "That invitation includes you, Ms. McAllister." Cameron glared, but Max ignored him. "We wouldn't want you to get the impression that Blackmore Inc. is just a man's club. We welcome women into all areas of our business."

Jackson rolled her eyes, smiling. "Noted. But no thanks."

Cameron was going to strangle Max if he had to listen to his friend harass Jackson for another minute.

"Suit yourself," Max said easily. "Cam?"

Derek gave Cameron a wary look and clapped Max on the back. "He'll catch up with us if he wants to." The three men nodded to Cameron and disappeared into a taxi. Leaving him standing with Jackson.

"Is Max ever serious?" she asked.

Cameron shrugged. "Occasionally. A couple things get under his skin." Like the subject of his family. And Natasha. In the time that Cameron had known Max, those were the only two subjects he had ever seen his friend get heated about.

Jackson tilted her head and looked at him. "Do you mind if I walk with you a bit?"

Of course he minded. It meant every ounce of his energy was going toward not touching her. Not watching her soft, full lips as she spoke in that husky voice.

But if he said no, he was an asshole. Correction: he was already an asshole. But he didn't need to make the situation worse.

Cameron sighed. "I was going to walk over to Haymarket for some dumplings. You're welcome to join me."

She hesitated. "Um, okay."

He nodded his head down the street. "This way. It's a bit of a walk."

Jackson smiled and pointed to her feet. "I bought a new pair of walking shoes."

Cameron made the mistake of looking down at them. He didn't know shit about women's shoes, and these looked roughly the same as any other pair. But of course he didn't stop his observations at the shoes. His gaze lingered at her ankles before tracing the curve of her legs up to the hem of her skirt. Today's was just short enough to get him thinking about her thighs. Shit.

Cameron shoved his hands in his pockets and started walking. Jackson caught up a moment later.

"Listen," she said breathlessly, "I just wanted to thank you for putting in the effort today with UNHCR. I talked with the director for a while before you got there, and he was beyond thrilled about the exposure."

Cameron nodded.

"He said that donations come in at times of crisis, but the money tends to dry up when the crisis is no longer on the front pages," she continued. "Something like this brings people's attention back."

Cameron glanced at her as she spoke. Her cheeks were flushed, and she was gesturing with her hands like she actually cared about what she was saying. Her eyes were alive. And she looked beautiful.

He raised an eyebrow at her. "You already got me in front of the camera. You don't need to sell me the idea anymore."

Jackson stopped in the middle of the busy sidewalk and put her hands on her hips. Cameron turned and met her gaze, and he found more than a hint of irritation in it. The lunch crowd bumped around her, but she didn't seem to care.

"I'm not selling anything, Cameron. Raising money for a good cause is important."

Cameron crossed his arms. "If that's what you feel strongly about, then why are you working in corporate PR, for companies like my father's?"

There. He'd said it. This was the question that had irked him since she'd shown up in his office for the first time. Why had she taken a job with Harlan?

Jackson's arms fell from her hips, and she looked away, frowning.

"That's complicated," she said.

Cameron took a step closer. "We're long past complicated, Jackson. I'd like to know."

"It's personal," she said, still not looking at him. "You know, you're just as much a threat to my job as I am to yours."

He blinked. All this time he had worried about her leveraging her power over his job, and she had been anxious about the same thing? That he'd use sex to manipulate her somehow? Cameron's shoulders fell. It was just the kind of thing Harlan Blackmore would do.

He uncrossed his arms and she turned to meet his gaze.

"I'd never use our personal time together against you. Or anything else personal, for that matter," he said softly. "Do you really think I would?"

His heart thumped in his chest as he waited for her judgment. Groups of people jostled by, but neither of them moved. Jackson held his gaze, her eyes searching his. She brushed a few strands of hair off her face.

"No, I don't think you would," she finally said. "Maybe I thought so at first, but not anymore."

He was dying to kiss her right now, no matter who was watching. But he didn't want to stop at a kiss. One encounter with her had left him reeling, and the second had left him desperate. Cameron wasn't sure he'd survive another with his sanity intact.

He lifted his hand to touch her but stopped and let it fall. Her eyes flashed with something—disappointment?—but she averted them and started walking.

"I took a job at a PR firm because I needed the money," she said flatly. "The nonprofit I started out with could barely afford my salary, and I needed double what they were paying me to move out of my sister's spare bedroom."

"And the firm you're at now doesn't take on nonprofits?"

"They do, but those accounts don't pay as well. So I started to go for other accounts, bigger ones like Blackmore Inc." She wrinkled her nose. "See, I'm on this ten-year plan…"

He raised his eyebrows.

"Long story," she said. "Anyway, I needed the extra money quickly, and they were looking for someone who would travel internationally. So I took it."

She needed the extra money quickly? The hair rose on the back of his neck, and his hands tensed into fists. How the hell did he ask his next question?

"Were you in some kind of trouble?" He frowned. He'd asked the question much more forcefully than he had meant to.

Jackson shook her head. "Not really. Just the plain old cheating boyfriend kind of trouble," she said. "So I needed my own apartment."

"Oh." Cameron unclenched his hands, and he rubbed his knuckles. "I'm sorry. That's crap."

She gave him a wry smile. "Yeah. I'm sorry, too. Good apartments are hard to find in New York."

Cameron smiled a little.

"You want to know something else?" She looked at him, and he slowed his pace. Her voice sounded less sure. "He's the reason I took you up to my room that first night. He had some…performance problems."

"And you suspected I wouldn't?"

"Well, yeah." Jackson laughed for real this time. "But he also told me that I didn't know how to have fun." Her smile faded a little.

"And he said you were causing his performance problems?" he asked slowly.

Jackson swallowed. "He didn't come out and say it. But he let me know that he didn't have any problems with the woman he'd cheated on me with."

What an asshole. He hissed out a breath. The dickhead was probably lying, too, but Cameron didn't want to push the subject. Jackson looked hurt, and he had to shove his hands into his pockets to keep from taking her into his arms.

They stopped on a corner at a red light. The crowd closed in on them, and he took a step closer to her.

"You know that's not true, clearly not true," he said softly.

Jackson shrugged. "I guess I do now." She looked lost in thought for a moment. "Yep," she added. "Those nights were definitely fun."

She started across the street with the rest of the crowd, leaving Cameron behind. Fun? This wasn't a deliberate insult, the way she had played *mediocre* the other night. *Fun* was ordinary, forgettable. Not something that kept Jackson up late at night or woke her up needy and aching for his mouth and his arms and his cock. And Jackson McAllister was not going home thinking they'd had *fun* together. In fact, he was starting to hope she wasn't going home at all.

She reached the other side of the street and turned around, looking for him, her brow creased. But when she found him in the crowd, her mouth tipped up into a slow smile, as if she'd found exactly what she was looking for. As if he were exactly what she wanted.

Cameron's heart pounded in his chest, and he quickened his pace. Maybe he still had a chance to sort this out. But how much progress could he make in a week?

CHAPTER NINE

JACKSON STOPPED IN front of Cameron's office door and took a calming breath. She had managed to get through the last few days without succumbing to the temptation of his godlike body. With effort, she'd stayed cool in yesterday's meeting as Cameron gave her the basics of the security job she'd shadow at an upscale gala. She'd get through this meeting, too.

The problem was the longer she went, the more time she spent thinking up reasons why she should stop resisting and get one more taste of Cameron before she left. And if she was going to have another no-strings night, there were a few more ideas she was interested in exploring. Judging from the way she caught him looking at her these past few days when no one else was around, he wouldn't turn her down.

It wasn't the sex itself she was wary of. But every time they were close, she started reading into all the little things he did. Like remembering what she liked on her sandwich or how she liked her coffee. As if it all meant something more.

But if she could just accept this for what it was—a

fling—she could invite him back to her hotel room again. Tonight. Because three nights together weren't worse than two. Nor were four nights. Or five.

And just like that, she flashed back to that first night, her heart pounding as she stepped into her room. With Cameron behind her, his harsh breaths in her ear, she thought she'd explode before she even got her clothes off. And then there was his apartment, when he'd buried his face between her legs and made her pant and scream.

The heat rushed up the back of her neck. Maybe the problem was that she was remembering these two nights as better than they really were. After a dry year, she must have been hard up. Cameron had stepped in at the right time. Times. And now she'd spent every night since thinking about it. Inflating each time in her mind. If she invited him up to her room for one more night, maybe reality would break this spell, and she could go back to New York satisfied in every way.

More rationalization.

Jackson brushed out the wrinkles in the front of her skirt and stared at the plaque on the door in front of her. *Cameron Blackmore, CEO*. As if she needed a reminder of who she would find on the other side when she opened it.

She knocked. "Mr. Blackmore?" Jackson peeked her head in. Cameron was facing his computer. His hair had fallen down on his forehead again, begging for someone to come fix it. Lots of ex-military men still wore their hair close-cut, but Cameron's thick black hair curled around his ears, and she had gotten a good handful of it that night when he... Nope. Shouldn't be thinking about that at all.

Jackson cleared her throat. "Mr. Blackmore, I just wanted to show you that the interview ran today."

He turned to her, and his gaze wandered down, stopping at the open neckline of her shirt. Yep, she had his full attention now. His gaze snapped back up, and his lips formed a tight line.

"Please don't call me Mr. Blackmore."

"Right. Cameron," she said, pulling out her laptop. Hopefully she could keep herself from blushing every time she said his first name.

Jackson opened her laptop on his desk and pulled up a chair beside him. She clicked on the article and a photo appeared of Cameron, Derek, Simon and Max outside the office building, all dressed in black suits and white shirts. They all looked good. And Cameron looked really good.

"The suits were a nice touch, Jackson," he said. "Thanks."

She smiled. "You're welcome. The reporter seemed to like you all. You're lucky. Some of those answers you gave could've been spun in other directions."

Cameron narrowed his eyes. "Spun? It's none of anyone's business why refugee organizations are my giving choice. And you know what I said was true. I finally made it public because someone convinced me that it might bring more money to UNHCR." He gave her a pointed look and added, "That's you, in case you don't remember."

Jackson rolled her eyes. "Got it. But I meant the other questions. About the women and the less-than-flattering media attention you've gotten lately."

Cameron pushed his chair back and leaned forward, resting his forearms on his knees. "That was true, too," he said. "We serve our clients well."

Jackson snorted—case in point. But the heat rushed to her face again. Hearing that comment from him shouldn't sting. She knew what he meant, but she couldn't help but think about all the women he'd been with. The press clippings suggested there'd been many, and though Cameron had said they didn't show the whole story, his reputation wasn't a complete lie, either. It was the reason she'd been sent here in the first place. "That sounds like an admission of guilt. You're lucky that guy didn't run with it."

Cameron turned his head, and his gaze was heated. "Are you trying to ask me a personal question?"

The right answer was "no." She was here in his office to talk about the interview she had set up for him. Which he had handled just fine. The rest shouldn't matter...but reading about his implied sexual exploits on the front page of a top business site didn't feel good.

Jackson closed her eyes. "I guess it's personal. I want to know...how much does the media have right about you?"

Cameron expelled a breath slowly. "I never sleep with active clients. I'm not my father."

She blinked her eyes open in surprise. "No, you're not at all. At least not from what I know of him."

Cameron was a clear copy of his father physically, but that was where the similarities ended. While Harlan Blackmore projected a glossy polished exterior, Cameron seemed to want to wear his roughest edges on the outside, for everyone to see.

"Look, my father paraded my mother around like he was a good, married man. My mother thought they were in love. But really he was fucking anyone he wanted, and he moved on when it was good for business. It was all for show. But I didn't find that out until a lot later." Cameron looked at her again. "I'd rather people think the worst of me than lead them on."

"Lower the expectations?"

He gave a humorless laugh. "I guess so." He ran a hand through his hair. "It's not like I never see any action, but it's rarely anything more than one…encounter. And always separate from business. Unless some sexy New Yorker catches me unaware."

"Catches *you* unaware?" Jackson snorted. "You found me at the bar, not the other way around."

Cameron shook his head slowly. "I know. That's not what I meant."

"I get it," she said. He raised his eyebrows at her, and she added, "But you prefer flings. You're not the relationship type."

"I said that, didn't I?" he muttered. "I haven't been for a long time."

"Just keeping the situation clear," she said quickly. "Got it."

Cameron turned to face her. He rested his arm on

the back of her chair and leaned closer. "Maybe I need to revise that statement."

Jackson put her hand up. "Not on my account."

"It's my statement," he murmured. "I can do whatever the hell I want with it."

Jackson hadn't breathed in way too long. Her breath came out as a little gasp, and she glanced over at Cameron to see if he had heard it. He definitely had.

"Ready?" he said, leaning closer. "If I got together with someone for more than just a night or two, it would be fun and intense and hot as hell in bed. And it wouldn't be anyone else's business except for mine and hers. And there definitely wouldn't be anyone else for either of us." He paused, playing with a strand of her hair. "You let me know if you want more details."

Jackson's heart was thumping way too hard. He didn't have to spell that part out for her. She didn't need to be told that getting together with Cameron Blackmore would be fun and intense and hot as hell. And after trying to stop obsessing over him for the last few days, she knew better than to rule anything out.

"What kind of details?" she whispered.

His eyes widened, and his mouth curved into a slow smile. "The kind we need to lock my door for."

Jackson's phone rang, and they both startled. Cameron straightened up, and Jackson reached into her bag and looked at the screen.

"Kyle?" Cameron's eyebrows shot up, and he frowned. She stood and took a couple steps away.

"Jackson, I forwarded you a couple emails to look at," her assistant said when she answered.

Shooting a glance behind her, she whispered, "Can I call you back in a bit?"

"Did I interrupt something? Sorry."

Jackson's face burned. "No, you didn't interrupt."

Her back was turned to Cameron, but she could practically feel the tension radiating from him.

"Nothing urgent," said Kyle. "It's late here, so just check your messages and I'll look at it in the morning."

"Okay."

Jackson hung up the phone and touched her heated cheeks. Damn. Kyle had cut them off before she'd done anything stupid. She should be regretting the first steps down the slippery slope of increasingly forbidden territory, but the regret wasn't coming. Just disappointment. She still wanted him, long after her rational brain should have kicked in.

Slowly, Jackson turned around. Cameron's mouth twisted into a scowl. "Who's Kyle?"

She blinked. Kyle? It took a moment to register his tone. Was it…jealousy? She smiled a little, and Cameron's expression darkened.

"Kyle's my assistant," she said. When the scowl didn't ease, she added, "He'd be more interested in you than me, Cameron."

He let out a breath and his shoulders came down an inch or two. A strange look crossed his face, as if his own reaction had taken him by surprise. Then the tension in his gaze turned hot, setting off a new kick of heat through her body.

She turned away.

"Where are you going?" he growled.

"To lock the door."

Jackson crossed the room on wobbly legs. Hopefully she'd make it to the door without tripping. They could do this just one more time. But who was she kidding? Hell, if he was going to strip her down right here, she'd probably come back for more. Again and again until her time in Sydney was up. And she could save all the issues with hooking up with him for the plane ride back.

Jackson faced him. He leaned back in his chair, legs splayed, not bothering to hide his growing erection. His dark gaze was doing crazy things to her insides.

"Does anyone have a key?"

Cameron smiled darkly. "Derek, Max and Simon. Why? You have some discovery fantasies you want to tell me about?"

A pulse of heat ran from her core. Did she have discovery fantasies, or was it just the sound of his voice right now? Everything he said sounded dirty.

Jackson had spent the last few days looking anywhere but at Cameron. Now, finally, she could look. Drink in his deliciously large body. His blue dress shirt was rolled up at the sleeves, revealing corded muscles and a spray of dark hair down his arms and on his big hands. It was the same color as the hair on his chest and the hair that trailed down his stomach. His washboard stomach. His shirt only hinted at it, but her memory was more than adequate.

If things were different, if they were together or even lived on the same continent, would she ever get used to being with such a physical man? Would she take him for granted? Or would she forever be fascinated by the power he held in himself? Damn, this man was too much. He brought his hand to the bulge in his pants and adjusted himself. Wait, how long had she been staring at his erection?

Her gaze snapped back up to his face, and he chuckled. "You can look all you want, sweetheart. I don't mind. And the way you lick your lips every time you look down at my pants makes me hard as hell."

She'd just licked her lips? Jackson closed her eyes. There was nothing to do but laugh. "I didn't realize I was that obvious."

"Believe me, I'm not complaining. But you might not want to do that in public."

"Right. Got it."

But as Jackson watched him from across the office, his smile faded. All the teasing was gone. His gaze raked down to the neckline of her shirt, over her hips, down her legs. Now it was his turn to stare at her. But that didn't last long. He stood up and came to her in fast strides. She took a step back and found the door behind her.

Cameron's gaze was raw and hungry, but he didn't touch her. He rested his hands on both sides of her, caging her in, his heavy body hanging over hers. Heat radiated everywhere from him, and it was impossible to tell where her breaths ended and his began.

His voice was a low rumble in her ear. "You still haven't answered my question. Do you have any fantasies you want to tell me about?"

She shook her head slowly. Not exactly fantasies. Curiosities.

"If it's not discovery, what makes you hot, Ms. Jackson McAllister?" He shifted closer. "What about office fantasies? Fantasies about everything we shouldn't be doing right now?"

She nodded slowly. Yes, she certainly had those. She hadn't thought about this kind of thing before she came to Sydney, but since she'd stepped into Cameron's office that first day, her imagination had become more and more...vivid.

He slid one hand behind her neck and she trembled as he wove it into her hair. She was starving for him, and now that he was so close, touching her, she couldn't wait any longer.

"You promised me details." She sighed. "About what it would be like..."

He smothered a grin when she couldn't finish her sentence. "Don't worry, Jackson. I haven't forgotten. I'm just making sure we're both on the same page."

Then finally, finally, he lowered his lips to hers. He was hungry, so hungry, and she was, too. She nipped at him and opened her mouth for luscious, lingering strokes of his tongue. She grabbed on to his hips and pulled him against her, and his hand tightened in her hair. She finally came up for air, and he eased back until their lips were barely touching.

"We're getting way ahead of ourselves," he panted. "Let's start back when you came into my office."

Were they going to play out this scenario, right here during work hours? This was a dangerous mix of real and pretend. What would happen if she played out the dirty office fantasies she had about Cameron? What if they were no longer just fantasies but things they really did together? Maybe it didn't matter. She was leaving soon, no matter what they did here. She tipped up her head, and her cheek brushed against the stubble of his chin.

"You wanna hear how I imagine this little meeting between us today, sweetheart?" he whispered. "I'm thinking you're not just here for two weeks. I'm thinking you work for me. You'd come in just like you did today. You'd lean over to show me whatever the fuck you wanted me to see, and you'd give me a nice view down your shirt, just like you did the first day you were here in my office."

Her eyes flared and he laughed. "And you'd give me that innocent, wide-eyed look, just like right now. I'd get hard, just like this." He took her hand and pressed it against his rock-hard erection, straining against his pants. "You ready to keep playing this out?"

"Yes." Hell, yes.

"So why don't we go back over to my desk and take it from there."

His fingers slid from her neck to her cheek before

he let his hand drop. Jackson slipped away from his body. He was right behind her, close enough to hear his breathing. Her heart pounded harder.

I'm thinking you're not just here for two weeks. I'm thinking you work for me.

How much was fantasy, and how much was about making sense of what they really wanted to be true? No, she wasn't going there. Act now. Analyze later.

She reached the desk, and he rested a hand on her hip. She drew in a sharp breath. Heat lingered everywhere he touched her. Where would they take this?

"You look fantastic today, Ms. McAllister," he whispered in her ear from behind her. "I'm so glad you came by my office." His hand made a slow trail over her shoulder and down her back. Lower. "You have a glorious ass," he muttered. "Last night when I came home, I got myself off in the shower imagining you against this desk, bare for me."

She could see him in his shower, his huge body shaking as he stroked himself. A rush of pleasure ran through her, and she moaned.

He traced the curve of her rear and continued down until he found the slit of her skirt. His hand touched the inside of her thigh, and she gasped. His laugh was soft and low.

"You've been wearing skirts like this all week," he said, reaching higher. "You know what I've been wondering? If I can just lift a skirt like this up whenever I want you, or if you'd have to take it off."

He inched her skirt up until his hand was between

her legs. *Please, just a little more.* No. She wasn't going to beg.

"Looks like I got my answer," he said, moving her panties aside. "And you're already so wet."

He played with her. Her head sank and she braced herself on his desk, legs shaking as his fingers teased and tempted.

"You've spent the last week telling me what you think I should do and how I should do it," he said. "And you seem to like that. I wonder how far you're willing to go to convince me."

Jackson closed her eyes, letting his hand and his voice fill her. She'd never fully understood the appeal of role-playing before. But whatever this was that they were doing right now was really getting her going. Her breasts tingled, aching to be touched.

"Are you willing to suck my cock?" he asked. "Because I'd agree to just about anything to have your soft, wet mouth around it again."

Oh, God. Her heart was pumping hard, and her words were stuck in her throat. What was wrong with her? She'd never truly want her job to depend on sucking off her boss. So why did playing like this with Cameron turn her on? Because she knew he'd never really force her? Something about this set her free to explore this scene, and she wasn't going to try to make sense of it.

"Is that what you want from me, Mr. Blackmore?" she asked. "You want me ready and willing when you ask for something?"

His fingers left her, and he pulled her hips back

against his erection and gave a slow, teasing thrust. He pressed his lips on the back of her neck.

"You know what I like, Jackson," he whispered. "And there's no one else I want it from."

Jackson. When he spoke her name, the game shifted into something else. She turned around and met his eyes. For a moment, neither of them moved. Raw heat blazed from him, something real and vulnerable. This was more than just getting each other off on dirty fantasies. A part of this was real for him, too. And she had no idea what to do with that.

"I'd like to give you whatever you want, Mr. Blackmore," she said, soft and husky.

Whatever was in his look just moments before disappeared. Lust sharpened his expression.

"Then get on your knees and give it to me."

He let go of her and eased back against his desk, spreading his legs a little, watching her the whole time. She knelt down on the floor in front of him. Thank goodness his office was carpeted. Jackson unbuckled his belt and unzipped his pants. His erection surged forward, straining against his boxer briefs.

"Take it out," he whispered.

She slipped her hands under his waistband and pulled it down, revealing his cock, huge and ready. She trembled, fighting to take this slowly, to tease out all the pleasure they could get from their little game. She closed her hand around him, and he let out a low groan.

"Is this how you like it, Mr. Blackmore?"

"Hell, yes," he bit out.

She smiled and put her mouth on his tip. She teased him with her tongue and her lips and then took in a little more.

He seemed to love this kind of play, having her push the limits of his control and then doing the same to her. It had been that way back at his apartment, and she'd loved being the one who got him off. Today they were playing that she was the only one he wanted to do these things with. Which was even better.

She experimented with her teeth as his knuckles grew whiter on the edge of the desk. His hisses of pleasure grew louder until he thrust once in her mouth.

"That's enough," he choked, urging her head back.

He helped her to her feet. Were they still playing? She didn't care anymore. All she could think about was him sinking inside of her, again and again. She was still fully dressed, and so was he, aside from his erection jutting out at her, calling for attention.

"You like this part of your job, Ms. McAllister?" he whispered. "You like driving a man like me to the point where all I can think about is coming inside of you?"

His eyes were wild, but he didn't move to touch her.

"Yes," she breathed, playing along. "I want to get you so hot you don't want it from anyone else but me."

Cameron stilled. He cupped her chin with his large hand and brushed his lips over hers.

"I'm already there, sweetheart," he whispered, drawing his fingers over her skin. He rested his hand at the base of her neck. "Now we're going to fuck until you're there, too."

He held her gaze, his eyes intense and demanding. She shifted, trying to control the burning need inside. She wanted everything Cameron would give her. She wanted to feel this fire between them explode.

Jackson tried to steady her voice. "Do you want me on the desk, Mr. Blackmore?"

She moved next to him and faced his desk. She looked over her shoulder through her lashes. His eyes narrowed, and he clenched his jaw. He pushed off his desk and came behind her.

The current sparked so strong between them. It would be fast and rough. She wanted it like that. But he held back. He inched her skirt up until it was around her waist and caressed her hips slowly.

"You like it this way, too, don't you?" he whispered in her ear.

"Yes, Mr. Blackmore."

"You want to please me."

"Yes, Mr. Blackmore," she breathed again.

"How far would you go to please me?" he said, even softer.

Jackson swallowed. "Anything you want." She knew that was true, whether this was a game or not. She also knew Cameron was the only man she'd say that to. He ran his finger under her panties. Then he reached between her legs, slowly exploring, before he pulled his wet fingers farther back and they skimmed between her two cheeks.

She shivered. She'd been curious about this since the

first time he offered. But should they try it right now, in his office, in the middle of the workday?

"I want to try," she whispered.

A pause. "You've never done anything here before," he said, his voice barely there.

She shook her head slowly. "No, but I want to, Mr. Blackmore." Before he could react, she pressed her hips back into his finger and gasped. *Whoa.* The sensation was strange...different.

Cameron's laugh was dark, and he pulled back. "I think that's as far as we'll go today. We'll try more next time."

Her body was molten liquid inside. Was it the power game or his finger or something else? Before she could decide, his hands were skimming down her legs, easing her panties off. He stuffed them in the pocket of his pants.

He opened the drawer of his desk and pulled out a condom, then he tore off the wrapper. Wait, he kept condoms in his office drawer? The thought reeled through her mind and took hold as she waited for him to put it on. Jackson couldn't shake it. She turned to face him, and he stopped, midprocess.

"Have you done this before, Cameron? Here?"

He blinked, as if he were taking her in anew. Slowly, he shook his head. "No." He paused. "You want to be the only one to do this with me, Jackson?"

Yes, she did. Cameron was waiting for her, but she

didn't answer. Instead she turned around and tipped her hips up.

"I'm ready, Mr. Blackmore."

CHAPTER TEN

CAMERON SQUEEZED HIS eyes shut, trying to screw his head back on after the last mind-blowing turn of events in his office. He was going to come in about five seconds if he didn't calm the hell down.

Was he really letting go of every last shred of sense just for one more glorious time with Jackson? This thought had run through his mind more than once, but he couldn't stop himself. All the hot tension of being close to her every day was short-circuiting his brain. And the insane jealousy that flashed through him as he listened to her call.

Then she had asked about the condoms. Which he had bought just for her, in case she changed her mind. She wanted it that way—just for her.

They were in dangerous territory. This was all supposed to be play, but it wasn't anymore. Not for him. And he was almost sure it wasn't for her, either.

...So hot you don't want it from anyone else but me.

Her words rang through him as he guided himself into heaven.

"Fuuuuuuck," he groaned, and she tilted her hips into his.

He was going to make way too much noise if he wasn't careful. His heart was already pounding at heart-attack speed. He moved as slowly as he could.

"Harder," she demanded, her voice needy and desperate.

She moved against him, and he gave her what she asked for. Again and again.

"Cameron," she cried.

He really might not make it through this. He'd die with his pants down, newly emptied, and he didn't even care. He should care, and he probably would later. But right now, that didn't matter.

He gritted his teeth and reached in front of her, finding her clit and that rhythm that would set her off. The only thing that mattered was the two of them. It was all too much. She squirmed and with a muffled shout she came around him. With a growl he came hard, stars filling his vision until he found himself leaning over his desk, holding her.

Cameron gulped in breaths, too stunned to move. He stayed there, even after his heart began to slow. God-damn, he had almost passed out when he came.

"Wow," she finally said.

"Yeah. Wow."

He didn't want to let go of her. This whole encounter had been about playing with dirty fantasies, but he couldn't stop thinking about how many times he had slipped closer to real. And she had slipped, too. He was sure the moment she had called his name. *Cameron.*

But they couldn't stay there forever. He propped himself onto his elbows and kissed her along the jawline, then ran his hand over her soft curves.

"Let's sit down for a few minutes. Catch our breath," he murmured.

She nodded.

He disposed of the condom and cleaned up at the corner sink. Then he tucked his half-hard dick back into his pants and walked over to the couch to watch Jackson. She was lovely. All that velvety dark hair and her smart mouth and that little game they'd just played that got him off like nothing ever had. He leaned into the couch cushions and rested his arm along the back. He was so gone on this woman, who lived on the other side of the world. And was hired by the board. All he could think about was getting her to lay back in his arms so he could shut his eyes and pretend she was his for a few more minutes.

Jackson shimmied her skirt back down her delicious round thighs and rebuttoned her shirt. She walked over to the couch and sat on the edge, leaving way too much room between them. She turned to him and let her gaze fall over his chest, his arms, everywhere.

"You know, you're really built," she said. "I've never been with someone so…" She waved away the end of the sentence.

What had she thought to say? Cameron studied her smile, but he couldn't read it. "That a good thing?"

Her smile widened. "Yes, definitely."

"Then help yourself, sweetheart." He shifted, leaving room for her to rest on his shoulder. She blinked and furrowed her brow a little, but she moved closer. She rested her head on his chest, and he wrapped his arms around her.

She made a little humming noise as her chest rose and fell in a long, deep breath. Damn. This was just about perfect.

Jackson looked up at him. "I didn't take you for much of a cuddler."

Cameron snorted. "I'm not. And if this gets out, I'll never live it down."

Jackson laughed. "I didn't see any of this coming. When you first walked up to me in that bar, I had all sorts of ideas about what someone like you spent his time doing."

"Oh, yeah? Give me one of your ideas."

She squeezed his arm gently, letting her fingers linger on his biceps. "Personal trainer?"

He laughed and shook his head. "Sounds boring as shit."

"You're right. You'd definitely do something more exciting." She tilted her head and smiled. "I also came up with a couple macho sports like wrestling crocodiles."

He rolled his eyes. "Come on. That's not a real sport. That's the worst Australian stereotype out there."

She waved him off. "No way. I could see tourists

paying to watch you wrestle crocodiles. Though you'd have to fake an Australian accent."

"Would you pay to watch me wrestle crocodiles?"

Jackson tapped her chin. "Hmm...maybe. Would you have a shirt on?"

He laughed. "Would you want me to?"

She rested her head on his chest and he caressed her cheek. He closed his eyes and held her closer.

"Hey, crocodile man," she whispered.

"Am I supposed to respond to that?"

"Shouldn't we be working?" she asked.

He sighed and kissed her on the top of her head. "Yep."

She sat up, shifting out of his embrace, to face him. He rested his arm on the back of the couch again to stop himself from pulling her back against him.

"I'm not here for much longer." She frowned. "We need to be careful."

"Careful of what?"

Careful not to get caught or careful not to get too involved? The former he could handle, but the latter? Jackson didn't answer. Maybe that was a good sign. Cameron let his fingers travel over her shoulder, down her arm. "So tell the board you need more time."

"To fit in more sex with you?"

Cameron gave a little snort. "You're supposed to be in PR, sweetheart. If you want them to agree, you'll have to come up with something better than that."

She smiled a little. "I can't lie to the board," she said.

Cameron sat up. "Lie? It's not a lie that it would help to have you here."

She shook her head. Shit. He had just stupidly laid down all his cards and suggested she stay. And she wasn't even considering the idea.

"Never mind," he grumbled. "Let's get back to work."

CHAPTER ELEVEN

"You can't stare at her like that, mate," said Derek.

"I know," Cameron muttered.

Apparently he had been staring, as evidenced by the fact that he hadn't heard Derek come up from behind. Which was a bad sign. Cameron rubbed his forehead. He had walked out of his office for some reason, but he couldn't remember what it was. Because seeing Jackson in that same skirt today was driving him crazy.

Another bad sign.

He was dying for a repeat of the other day in his office, and just thinking about how he could lift this skirt over her hips was turning him on.

"You're getting in way too deep, Cam," muttered Derek. "Let's get back into your office before the sexual harassment police come by."

Cameron tore his eyes from Jackson's curves and ducked into his office. Derek shut the door and parked himself on the sofa. This guy wasn't leaving until whatever he had on his mind was said.

"All right, you wanker, what the hell do you think you're doing?"

Cameron sank into the sofa next to him and ran his hand through his hair. He blew out a breath. "I don't know. Something really stupid."

"Yep." Derek nodded. "Because you're staring at her like you're imagining her doing something dirty."

He couldn't stop himself. The moment Derek said those words, he flashed to the scene in his office just a couple days ago. When she'd bent over his desk for him and he'd taken her from behind. He let out a strangled sound of frustration.

"You fuckwit," whispered Derek. He shook his head. "You've already done it for real. Shit."

Cameron closed his eyes. "Remember that night in the hotel, when I told the three of you that it was our last night to have some fun? Of all the women in Sydney, I picked her up, okay? I had no idea. And it was good. I mean, really good. So much more than anything like that has a right to be." Cameron shook his head. "And I might have been able to let it be if she hadn't shown up in our office the next day, all buttoned up and wide-eyed."

Derek clapped him on the back a couple times. He actually looked sympathetic. "And now?"

"Fuck if I know," he said. "Every time I see her, it's like I can't tear myself away from her. Even when we're just sitting in the conference room, I find reasons to keep her talking, just so she doesn't leave. I can't help myself, okay?"

Cameron rubbed his hands over his eyes and let his

shoulders sag. "She's going to leave for real. Soon. And I don't know what the hell I can do about it."

"You sure she's not just playing with you?" asked Derek.

Cameron shook his head. "I don't think so. But I guess I can't be sure."

Derek leaned back into the sofa pillows, and he was silent for way too long. Not good. Derek was from one of the biggest families in the Samoan community in Sydney, and both his father and his grandfather were church leaders. Even though Derek had chosen a different path, people came to him with their problems all the time. And he was never silent.

He glanced over at his friend. "Well?"

Derek raised his eyebrows. "I don't know what you want me to say. You won't see a shrink to get over your flying thing. And she lives in New York. There are ten thousand miles of issues. Something's got to give."

"A shrink won't help," spat Cameron. "I can't do it. I can't get myself on a plane. I'm afraid I'll lose it in a way I'll never come back from."

He couldn't even think of airplanes without flashing back to that crash in the desert and the two men who'd never come back. It was still so real. The utter panic of knowing the engine had failed and they were falling... The impossible, jarring impact as one side of the plane hit the ground and went up in flames. The heat from the burning wreckage, the slashing pain in his midsection and the inhuman screams coming from the men. He closed his eyes against it all.

"You made it across the Pacific once. You can do it again," Derek said.

"Simon was with me," said Cameron. "Just ask him about that plane ride."

"Okay, okay," said Derek, his hands up in surrender. "So find another way to spend some more time with her."

"I suggested she ask the board for more time, but she didn't even consider it." Cameron grimaced. "She mentioned a ten-year plan. And she's got this little red book she writes in. If I could see it, I bet I could figure this out. But I'm not lifting it from her. I'm not stooping that low."

Or would he?

His friend patted his arm and stood up. "Sorry, mate. It doesn't sound good."

"No shit," he said.

Cameron walked Derek to the door and rested his hand on the knob. "There's got to be a way."

Derek smiled. "Cameron, Jackson's smart and beautiful, and she stands up to you. I probably shouldn't say this, but I've seen her looking at you when she thinks no one sees. If you want this badly enough, you're going to find a way to make it work."

"Thanks for nothing," he grumbled and opened the door.

And came face-to-face with Jackson McAllister.

"Oh." She gasped.

Shit. How much of their conversation had she heard? But she wasn't paying attention to him. She was peering into her little red book again. What the hell did she write in it?

Derek slipped by her with a nod, and then it was just the two of them. Alone.

"Ms. McAllister?"

Jackson stuffed the little book into her bag. "Right. Sorry."

Cameron covered her hand. She looked up at him, her lips parted as if she were ready to kiss him. Except that wasn't going to happen. Not here, in the Blackmore Inc. hallway.

"I've seen you pull that little book out a few times," he said softly. "Can I see it?"

"It's nothing," she said, but her face was bright red. "It's just a bunch of lists. Nothing interesting."

"I'm interested."

She glanced down the hallway. Derek had disappeared.

"Let's go into your office," she whispered. That shouldn't sound so seductive, but he must have reacted because she added, "Not for *that*."

Right. Take it easy.

Cameron stepped back, and Jackson walked into his office. She pulled up a chair to his desk and sat down. Leaning back against his desk, his legs were inches from hers.

Keep focused. The book. She had taken it out a few times, so it meant something. It had to be the key to figuring out her ten-year plan.

"What's in that book, Jackson?"

"Boring stuff," she said quickly. "Just places I want to go, things I want to visit."

"Can I see it? Please?"

Jackson looked up at him. "Okay. But promise not to laugh." She pulled it from her bag and handed it to him.

The cover was soft and worn, and some of the pages had come loose from the binding. He opened the book to the first page. *My Dream Trips* was underlined three times and surrounded by little hearts. He glanced up at Jackson, and she smiled.

"I got it when I was about twelve, in case you're wondering."

Cameron chuckled. "You never know."

"No laughing." She took a swat at his leg as he turned the page.

"'Paris,'" he read. "Of course. 'The Eiffel Tower, the Mona Lisa...' All the things you want to see there?"

"Yep. Some places have more details than others. I had to add another Paris page."

She took the book from him and flipped to a page in the middle. She handed it back to him.

"Rue Cardinale Lemoine? What's there?"

"Hemingway's apartment." She rolled her eyes. "College."

"Have you been to Paris?"

Jackson sighed. "Nope. Not yet." She flipped to the beginning, to the page titled New York. "Look here. I cross out everything I've done."

Cameron raised his eyebrows. "You still haven't seen everything you want to see in New York?"

Jackson smiled. "It's a big city. And I add to the list all the time. Restaurants I want to try, that kind of thing."

He nodded. "Does Sydney have a page?"

Jackson hesitated. She took the little book again and leafed through the pages. "No laughing, remember?"

The Opera House. Climb the Harbour Bridge. Bondi Beach. The list was long, and only two entries were crossed out. *Boat trip in the Sydney Harbour* and... *Hot sex in Sydney?* Cameron's mouth fell open. Should he be offended or flattered?

"Is that me?" he snorted.

He caught the smile on her face just before she buried her head in her hands. Finally, she looked up again. "That's you."

He pumped his fist in the air. "I made your list. Glad to see it's crossed off."

She pursed her lips.

He tried for a straight face but failed. "It's a little funny, isn't it?"

She smiled. "Okay. A little."

He looked down at her list again. The things that were crossed out she'd done with him. One was the night on his boat. While he spent the whole ride thinking about how to deal with her in his apartment, she was thinking about her dream list. Shit.

"You've only accomplished two things on your Sydney list?" He could have spent the last week and a half showing her all the things written there. They could have done them together.

He looked up at her. "That day we ate right on the harbor, you should have said something. We could have walked up to the Opera House."

Jackson shrugged. "I was working, remember? Besides, we're going to the Sydney Opera House in a couple days for the security job."

Cameron nodded. The private security detail at the gala. That was her last night in town. All he could think about was the time they had wasted. He'd spent so much of it thinking about getting her naked that he'd missed this whole piece of what she wanted. Not that she had complained about the getting naked part.

She took the book out of his hands and flipped through the pages. "It's not an itinerary. More like a fantasy life I want to live someday. When I have more money, and I'm not so busy with work."

She skimmed through pages on the French Riviera, Mont Saint-Michel and Marseille. She really had a thing for France.

"The ten-year plan?"

She sighed. "Yep."

"What about vacations?"

Jackson shrugged. "Sometimes. When I have the money." She flipped to a page titled St. Thomas, Virgin Islands. *Beach cabana* and *waterside restaurant* were crossed off, but *sailing trip* and *snorkeling* weren't. She looked up at him and gave a wry smile. "My ex-boyfriend wasn't into water sports, so we skipped some of the items."

What the hell was wrong with this guy? He had

Jackson all to himself on a Caribbean island, and he wouldn't get in the water with her? If Cameron had Jackson to himself, he'd do whatever the hell would make her happy.

Except get on an airplane, you fuckwit. Which means you can't give her any of the things she wants.

Cameron frowned. "Did your ex know about this book?"

"I guess. He saw me writing, but he never really asked about it." She closed it and stuffed it back in her bag. "It doesn't matter. Like I said, I'll probably never make it to most of these places. The lists are just for fun."

He studied her expression. No, this mattered to her. She had kept that little red book for years, adding new places all the time, waiting for a chance to start living her dream. This was what she wanted. But Cameron wasn't any better than her ex-boyfriend. At least the dickhead had actually gone somewhere with her. Cameron scowled and turned away.

"I know it's a little childish," she said quickly.

Was that what she thought was going through his mind? He was on the verge of screwing this up worse.

"It's not," he said, a little too forcefully. "That's not what I was thinking at all."

She tilted her head. "Then what were you thinking?"

"A lot of things. I wish I would have taken you to some places on your Sydney list."

Jackson's eyes were soft, and she smiled a little. She

paused, as if she were really considering it. "Maybe someday."

Someday. As in, probably never. Unless he figured something out.

CHAPTER TWELVE

WHEN THE ELEVATOR doors closed, Jackson hitched up the top of her dress and swiped a hand down the skirt. The black satin bodice still dipped dangerously low. The saleswoman in the department store had assured her that the dress wasn't too small. It was supposed to show a hint of cleavage. But Jackson was showing more than a hint. And it was too late to change her mind.

She folded the wide, silky scarf around her chest as the elevator raced up. Thank goodness she was leaving tomorrow. If she was around Cameron much longer, she might spontaneously combust. When the rest of his team was around, Cameron barely even looked in her direction. He was short with everyone, and when Max patted her on the shoulder, she could swear Cameron growled.

But when they were alone, it was worse. As soon as he came close, the electricity between them sizzled. Like he was silently waiting for her signal. And she couldn't stop herself from giving in to it.

The elevator dinged, and the doors opened to the top floor. She clutched the scarf around her shoulders tighter and stepped out. The reception desk was empty, but she could hear low voices coming from down the hall. Jackson took a deep breath.

How many fantasies had she flashed through these last days? Fantasies of giving in to the magnetic pull between their bodies for another euphoric encounter before she left. The tension between them built all day. When he read a memo over her shoulder or helped her with her coat, all she had to do was meet his liquid blue eyes. She found what she wanted.

Then, as soon as she got far enough away from the tractor-beam pull of his body, she could see this wasn't leading anywhere good. It was one thing to play out an office fantasy, but real life didn't work the same.

Still, as she'd stood in the boutique's changing room, shopping for an outfit for tonight, she knew the dress was more sexy than professional. And she bought it anyway.

Jackson looked down at the crumpled silk in her fists and sighed. Before she walked into the conference room full of testosterone, she needed to pull herself together.

She slipped the scarf off her shoulders and shook it out, but the wrinkles remained. She frowned. Maybe she could—

Footsteps, close by. Jackson lifted her gaze and found Cameron, only a couple paces away. He wore black dress pants and a white dress shirt with gun holsters strapped across his chest. Refined but dangerous. His eyes, dark and hungry, dipped down over every curve of her body. He rested his gaze on her cleavage with unrestrained lust.

Cameron took a step, closing in on her. Another step. She fought the urge to turn the tables on him, to back him against the wall and make the spark in his eyes explode. But this was work. He took one more step. His body was only inches away from hers, and when she took a breath, her breasts skimmed his shirt. Her heart did flips in her chest.

Cameron rested his hand on the wall and leaned over her. The scent of his aftershave took her right back to his living room couch as he drove deep inside her. God, she wanted him right now. A low rumble rose from his chest.

"What the *hell* are you wearing?" he whispered roughly.

She swallowed and straightened up.

"This is a formal event," she said, her voice far too breathless. "I'm trying to fit in."

"And you look sexy as fuck," he groaned. "You said you'd be out of the way, that I wouldn't even notice you. But you're putting far too much faith in my self-control if you think I can turn away when you look so fucking good in that dress."

His breath warmed her neck, and the heat from his body pulsed into hers. Or maybe it was her own body. She squeezed her hands into fists to keep herself from touching him. Just one more time. Once more, she wanted to run her hands over the muscles that strained against the fabric of his shirt. She shifted a little, and her hip brushed against him. His erection grew.

"We're working," he grumbled.

She waited for him to judge his next move. He stayed still.

His breaths rasped in her ear. "I'm going to walk back to my office and calm myself the hell down." He pressed his hard length against her hip, in case she wasn't sure what he was talking about.

His lips brushed against her neck. "Or you can follow me back there."

She closed her eyes, trying to steady her heavy breaths.

Then he was gone. Her eyes drifted open in time to see him turn around, his hands shoved in his pockets. He started down the short hallway. Shit. Just thinking of him in his office got her going. Was he going for the cold shower method of calming down, or was he getting himself off? He wouldn't, would he? She wanted to know.

If she followed him for the kind of quick, hard satisfaction she knew he could give her, it might make the night a lot easier. But she knew better than to follow him back before a key job for a little pleasure. Okay, a lot of pleasure. More than she'd probably ever get for the rest of her life. Double shit.

Jackson smoothed out the scarf she was clutching and wrapped it around her shoulders. Then she started down the hall. She got to the end and looked left, toward Cameron's office. His door was closed. Was he sitting at his desk with his pants unzipped, his big cock in his hand? Was he waiting for her? Damn. She was dying to walk down that hall and find out.

She looked to the right. The door to the conference room at the end of the hall was open. Derek Latu sat at the long table, his broad shoulders and his back just in sight. All he had to do was turn his head in time to see her slip into Cameron's office.

Jackson gave herself a little shake. Good God, what the hell was wrong with her? All Cameron had to do was lean over her, and she was panting after him like a puppy. She was a professional adult, not some hormonal teenager.

No more thinking about Cameron's big, hulking body or his intoxicating scent. She was not even going to turn around for another look at his office door. She was going to put one foot in front of the other and walk to the conference room. And not think about what she was missing back in Cameron's office.

Derek turned around just before she reached the conference room doorway.

"Cameron went out to find you," he said, raising an eyebrow. "You didn't see him?"

Jackson fought the heat rising to her face. "He had to take care of something. He'll be back in a few minutes."

Derek's gaze rested on her for an extra beat. He knew something was up. Thank goodness she'd come to her senses before she followed Cameron back and did something really stupid. Correction: something *else* really stupid.

She tugged her scarf across her chest and walked into the room. Derek and Max were dressed like Cameron: white shirts, black pants and holsters strapped around their shoulders. No wonder Blackmore Inc. was in such high demand. Both of them looked like they were ready for anything.

"Don't let me interrupt," she said.

Max glanced at her dress and laughed. "Good luck with that."

Jackson felt her face heat.

"Enough, Max," said Derek. "Let's review what Ms. McAllister needs to know."

She sat in the empty chair next to Derek, and Max passed her a paper across the table.

"Here's the schedule for the evening," he said. "In all likelihood, you'll see very little action on this job. But you never know. Because of some recent problems, this client suspects he's being targeted, and he's a little jumpy. He has his own full-time security back at the hotel, but he wants us along because we know the area."

She looked at the minute-by-minute plan, starting at an unnamed hotel.

"Who is the client?" she asked.

Derek shook his head. "Sorry. Can't give that information out."

"Fine," she said. "Where's Simon?"

Derek pointed to the top of her sheet. "He's already at the venue. Cameron will drive you there and get you into the place, and Max and I will pick up the client and his wife."

Which meant more time alone with Cameron. Her heart thumped.

Derek pointed farther down the timeline. "The client will stay for a couple hours, and then Max, Simon and I will take him back."

"And Cameron?" she asked.

"He'll take you back. He didn't want you near the client. In the unlikely event that anything would happen."

"Oh." Jackson frowned.

What was the board thinking when they insisted she tag along on their assignment? The more she thought about it, the more she suspected that Cameron was right. She was in the way. Hanging around on a job was risky, both for her and for the team, and Harlan Blackmore and his board had no idea what they were asking her to do. But Cameron did, and he had taken on the job of babysitting her.

Derek was still looking at her.

"He volunteered, Jackson," he said quietly. "He wanted to make sure you were safe." Derek punctuated his statement with a nod and turned back to Max for more planning talk.

Was Derek trying to tell her what a pain in the ass she was for Cameron, or was he saying something else? If it was the former, she didn't need any reminders. If it was the latter? It didn't matter. She was leaving tomorrow, so even if there was something more between them, there wasn't anything to do about it.

Derek and Max stopped talking, and Jackson looked up. Cameron stood in the doorway. His thick black hair was off his face, and his blue eyes were steely and cold. He wore a suit coat, unbuttoned. His hands were shoved into his pants pockets, showing hints of the now-loaded holsters around his shoulders. His eyes met hers, and for a moment, heat flared in them. Jackson drew in a breath, much louder than she meant to. Both Derek and Max looked at her, then back at Cameron. Shit. She had just all but announced her inappropriate interest in Cameron.

Max smiled at Cameron. "I think I better get out of here before I say something stupid."

Derek snorted. "That would be a first."

Max and Derek stood up and headed out the door. Max patted Cameron on the shoulder as he passed, shaking his head. The men's voices faded, leaving her alone with Cameron.

His gaze was steady on her. She wrapped her scarf tighter around her shoulders and stood up.

"You ready?" he asked, his voice rumbling from his chest.

"Yes."

Jackson tried hard not to stare as she passed him. She really did. But his muscular body in a well-tailored suit and armed...well, it was impossible to ignore. He was sex and danger, and he was watching her right now like nothing else in the world existed. Did he do this to every woman he slept with? If so, he must have a long line of stalkers still hung over from all the intense attention he poured on them. Good thing she was leaving tomorrow night. If she lived any closer, she might become one of those stalkers.

He stayed a half pace behind her, his large body looming just out of sight. He was on the job now, ready for anything. And yet the connection between them wasn't broken. Every rasp of his heavy breaths sent a current through her. Every brush of his arm against her flooded her with heat.

Jackson stopped in front of the elevator and pushed the call button. She stared at the doors, steeling herself for a painfully silent ride inside a small, private space. With Cameron.

The doors opened, and they stepped in. Jackson searched for something to say, something to ease the crackling tension between them.

"You don't have to chaperone me tonight, Cameron," she said, keeping her gaze on the elevator doors. "I'll be fine on my own."

"I won't hover over you, if that's what you're worried about."

"That's not what I mean." She turned and looked up at him. Some of the iciness in his eyes faded. "I'm sorry you had to plan me into your job, too," she said. "I'm sorry about this whole situation."

The heat flared in his eyes again. "I'm not."

Jackson blinked.

"I'm not sorry about anything that's happened between us, Jackson," he said.

His voice was low and heavy. Jackson bit her lip and turned to watch the floor numbers tick down. The truth was she wasn't sorry that they'd gotten together, either. Who would be sorry about scorching-hot sex? Nope, not sorry at all. It was the first time she had done anything this bold and quite possibly the last.

But why did it have to happen this way, when she was supposed to be working with him? Not even working. She was supposed to be training him. And reporting on him. And planning for future actions. Yes, she was doing her job, too, with good results so far, if the press they had gotten was any indication. But the mix of business and *so* not business was a dangerous game.

The elevator doors opened, and Cameron stepped out first, scanning the lobby. He was fully on guard, focused. He walked out first and then waited for her to pass. Her own private security.

A car waited for them at the building's entrance, and the driver helped her in. They rode in silence through the Sydney streets, past tall buildings, past restaurants and cafés, past Circular Quay, past couples enjoying the evening breeze. Cameron leaned back against the seat and looked out the window, his face blank and unreadable.

The car slowed as they approached the circular drive where the road officially ended and pulled onto the narrow path that led to the Opera House. The driver stopped a bit in front of it and opened her door, and she stepped out into the evening air.

The Sydney Opera House was a majestic building during the day, but at night, it was magical. Each rounded white peak glowed, and the interior lights shone through the tall windows of the front entrance, creating patterns of lines and shadows. The building was perched high up above the harbor, and a long red rug cascaded down the enormous mountain of steps to the entrance.

"Wow," she breathed.

Cameron's low voice came from close behind. "An amazing creation, isn't it?"

Jackson nodded. Her gaze dropped lower, and she eyed the stairs. Good thing she wore flats tonight, considering what they were here for. The store saleswoman had almost talked her into red heels.

As they started up the steps, she snuck a glance at Cameron. His face was blank, but his whole body was alert. Not tense, just aware. If the board ever saw him on the job, in this mode, they'd never think for a moment that he didn't take the business seriously.

Everything about him was impressive. And though she had resisted so many times that week, her resolve not to spend another night with him was crumbling. Yes, she read too much into sex with him. But tomorrow night she'd be on a plane back to New York, no matter what she read into it. And it wasn't like anyone would find out. The man was in security, for goodness' sake. He knew how to be discreet if he wanted to. Though the pile of photos in her file suggested otherwise.

Would these stairs never end?

"We can stop and rest a bit," said Cameron.

Jackson gave a little huff and nodded. They took another step and turned toward downtown. The sun was setting somewhere beyond the buildings, and the sky glowed with reds and oranges. The lights on the Harbour Bridge sparkled on the water, and the ferries glided in and out of Circular Quay.

She smiled and turned to Cameron, perched on the step below. For the moment, they were almost the same height.

"Is this in your little red book, Jackson?"

He could have been talking about the Sydney cityscape, which was, in fact, impressive. But he wasn't. She knew he wasn't. He was asking her, *Is this what you want?*

"It's not in there," she said, "but it probably should be."

She meant to give him her best business face, unfazed and assessing, but she couldn't. Maybe it was how close they were standing, his wide shoulders brushing against hers. Maybe it was the sunset, glowing behind the city. Maybe it was his soft, full lips that tasted like heaven. But as she met his eyes, his smile faded. Her heart stuttered.

No. She couldn't be falling for this man. Not Cameron Blackmore.

Jackson gulped in a breath. Cameron, raking his hand through his hair, turned away and checked his watch.

"The rest of the team will be here in about thirty minutes," he said. "I need to get inside and meet Simon."

His gaze was fixed on the entrance. Right. He had a job to do, and so did she. But for one delicious moment, she had let herself want him. Not just in bed. She wanted him for real. She had all her clothes on, so she couldn't blame it on a post-orgasmic haze. Damn.

She looked up at Cameron's face. Did she dare wonder if he wanted her, too?

But the moment was gone. The blank, focused expression he had worn since they'd walked out of the office was back. They finished mounting the stairs and, after being admitted into the event, stopped just inside the door.

"Where's Simon?" she asked. "Or are we using some kind of secret route?" She smiled up at him. He didn't smile back.

"We? *We're* not going anywhere." He frowned. "*I'm* going to meet Simon. *You're* going into the event."

Jackson put her hands on her hips. "You're not ditching me for the whole night while you go off and do your job. I'm here to watch how you work."

Cameron clenched his jaw. "You're PR, not quality control," he bit out. "You'll see enough from the event room."

What? After the last two weeks, did he still think he could bark at her like she was some disobedient child? This man knew how to piss her off like no one else did.

"Number one," she said, raising a finger in front of his face, "you're not calling the shots alone here, and you can't just cut me off. Number two, Derek said this wouldn't be dangerous. Number th—"

Cameron's enormous hand closed over hers before she could lift a third finger. "You remember what happened the last time you started counting things off for me."

Jackson's heart stuttered. His living room. Oh, yes, she remembered. And with his large chest just inches away, the scent of him all around... No. She pulled her hand away and glanced around. No one was looking. Thank God.

Cameron gave himself a little shake. He closed his eyes, and his chest rose and fell heavily. Finally, he looked at her.

"Okay, Jackson. I hear you." He sighed. "But I don't like this. You can come and get a sense of what's going on while I meet with Simon, but the moment the client gets close or anything else happens, you need to be far away. No questions."

Jackson blinked. Was Cameron Blackmore actually offering a compromise?

"All right." She put her hand on her hip. "That was easier than I thought."

Cameron gave an incomprehensible snort and pulled out an earpiece from the collar of his shirt. He murmured something into it, and after a beat, he took her hand. "Let's go."

They walked up a flight of stairs and down another. She snuck glances into doorways, trying to get a glimpse of the rooms in this iconic building, but after a while she gave up. Someday she'd come back here and take her time.

Cameron pushed through a door into an empty hallway, muttering short phrases, presumably to Simon. He didn't look in her direction, but he kept her hand tucked tightly into his. He stopped at every corner, ushering her behind him. Jackson tried to keep up with Cameron's long strides. She was starting to pant, but she wasn't about to ask him to slow down.

But as they turned down yet another hallway, Cameron stopped and mumbled something.

"Shit," he hissed, turning to her. "We have a problem. I need to get you out of here."

"Okay," she whispered.

Cameron glanced around and pointed at a door. "In there."

He put his hand on his gun and looked into the dark room. Jackson waited in the hall, listening to the noises in the distance. No one was in sight. He grabbed her hand again, and they slipped inside. The space was windowless, lit only from an open doorway along another wall.

"We'll be out of the way in here," he said, his voice low. "But we need to close that door. Stay close."

He led her across the room. But when they reached the doorway, Cameron froze. Jackson bumped into his side, but he didn't move a muscle. She opened her mouth to ask what was going on, but she heard why he must have stopped. Footsteps. Cameron whispered something. Simon must have said something back because his grip on her hand tightened. What was happening?

The footsteps grew louder. Cameron's grip on her hand grew to bone-crushing tight.

A shadow appeared outside the door. And the footsteps stopped. Shit.

"I'm so glad to finally get you alone," said Cameron loudly.

What?

"Go with it," he breathed when she didn't respond.

Oh. Now she got it.

"I've wanted you all night," she said.

"Come here, sweetheart." He backed her away from the hall and into the wall of the dark room, his big body shielding hers. Over Cameron's heavy breaths, the footsteps resumed. Closer. Cameron's fingers dug into her waist. "Don't worry. No one will find us here."

The footsteps stopped again. Then there was a crash. Cameron froze, but he didn't pull away.

Grunts came from the hallway. Cameron shifted, and his arms wrapped around her, holding her against him. His heart pounded in his chest, just as hard as hers.

More grunts. Then came a voice. "All clear."

Simon.

Cameron's lips brushed the top of her head before he let her go. "Stay here," he murmured to her.

He walked to the doorway and stopped. "You look like shit."

"He looks worse," said Simon. "Looks like we earned our keep before the event even started."

Cameron shook his head. "Nice job. Let Max and Derek know."

Jackson took a step forward, but Cameron put out his hand.

"Derek and Max are just around the corner," said Simon. "Go. Take her back."

Cameron gave a curt nod and came back to her. Curiosity was getting the better of her. Just how bad did Simon look? But one glance at Cameron told her that she'd have to leave it to her imagination. He took her hand and headed for the far entrance, where they had come in.

When they walked out, she stopped. "That was the guy you were supposed to look out for?"

Cameron nodded. "One of them."

"That was...close," she whispered.

He nodded, and the corners of his mouth turned down. He reached for her face and brushed his thumb over her cheek.

"You didn't want me to see that guy?" she asked.

"Not that. I didn't want him to see your face."

Oh. She really had no idea what she was getting into.

"I'm sorry," she said softly. "I really shouldn't be here."

Cameron didn't answer. He wrapped his arms around her once again and pulled her in tight. Heat radiated from his body, and desire spiraled in the wake of all the excitement.

"We need to get you back to the event," he said gruffly.

CHAPTER THIRTEEN

CAMERON RUBBED HIS palms over his eyes and gave himself one more little shake. Thank God this night was almost over. He watched two big black cars drive away from the side exit of the Opera House. He had gotten through the event, but just barely.

What the hell was wrong with him? He had stupidly let Jackson come along to give her what she wanted. To please her. Instead of following his instincts and keeping her away from all potential danger.

Thank God the rest of the job had gone smooth and easy. Security was already tight at this event. The politician who had hired them wasn't the only high-profile guest, and even getting Jackson a ticket had been a stretch. They needed to figure out how the hell that guy had slipped in.

He couldn't shake the mistake, even long after he left Jackson perched on a stool at one of the cocktail tables. This was why he kept his dick in his pants when it came to business. His grandfather never would have let a woman cloud his judgment. So why he still couldn't get Jackson out of his mind, even after he'd screwed up, was too much to process as he walked back into the Bennelong Room.

The lights were dim in the grand, cathedral-like space, and the wooden walls glowed in a warm yellow hue. The bar was a raised area in the middle, and he stopped there to survey the scene. The place usually served as a restaurant, but the dining tables were gone, replaced with a few cocktail tables and a wooden dance floor in the middle. A handful of couples danced, and the rest clumped together in groups, deep in conversation.

He found Jackson immediately. She was standing right where he'd seen her last, at a round cocktail table, and from this angle he got an eyeful down the front of her dress. Unfortunately, Cameron wasn't the only one who was enjoying the view. A man set a drink in front of her, and that guy's gaze dipped down more than once.

He started down the stairs and headed straight for her. Her eyes met his as he approached, and she held his gaze for one long, drawn-out moment before she looked back at the wanker who was talking away, his back to Cameron.

"Sounds to me like your date forgot about you," the guy continued. "I'd be happy to take you out on the dance floor if he has something better to do. But to tell you the truth, I can't think of a single excuse for a man not to show a beautiful woman like you a good time tonight."

Cameron stopped within range of a good jab. "Is that so?"

The guy turned around, and his eyes flared open. Cameron didn't love to use his size to intimidate, but this asshole was asking for it.

"Sorry, mate," the guy mumbled and backed away, leaving Cameron alone with Jackson.

"Was I interrupting something?" he growled. Real charming. He had to pull himself together. Had he really sunk as low as petty jealousy?

But Jackson just rolled her eyes. "He's harmless. He just wanted to dance."

"What he wanted was to get a look down your dress," he said drily.

Jackson sighed, and Cameron bit back a curse. He wasn't going to mess this night up. Not with Jackson standing in front of him in the sexiest dress he had ever seen. She could have worn some uptight business suit tonight. Instead, she'd worn that dress knowing they'd go to this event together. Knowing he'd see her in it.

"Are you off the clock?" she asked.

Cameron nodded and looked out at the dance floor. A man a little older than him was holding a beautiful woman in a long red dress. His hands rested on her hips as they moved slowly to the music. He leaned down and whispered something in her ear, and the woman turned to him and smiled like he was the only thing that mattered in the world.

It had been a shitty night, and all Cameron wanted was to hold Jackson like that right now. He wanted to breathe in her scent and feel her breasts against his chest. Hell, he wanted a lot more than that, but at this point, he was desperate enough to settle for a dance. And he hated dancing. This was only more evidence of how screwed up in the head he was over this woman.

"I'm so sorry I was in the way tonight," she said.

He frowned. "It's my job to deal with any circumstances that arise."

She was quiet. Cameron took a steadying breath and turned to Jackson. She was watching the other couples, too.

"You wanna dance?" he said roughly.

Jackson studied him for a moment. "Are you asking me?"

"Yes, I'm asking you."

Smooth, asshole.

"Sorry," he mumbled.

She glanced around the room, and he followed her gaze. It was a discreet crowd, used to attention, used to blocking out everyone else around them. Perfect. He took a step closer and ran his hand down the smooth, bare skin of her arm.

"We're surrounded by people with royal titles and Academy Awards. No one here gives a shit about you and me." He shoved his hands in his pockets. "If you want to dance, let's do it."

The corners of Jackson's mouth turned up. "You really are a charmer, Cameron Blackmore."

"So I've been told."

He could feel his own smile growing. Hell, he could stand here and talk to her all night just to hear the next sassy remark out of her mouth. But when she looked up at him, she hesitated. As Jackson's deep green eyes blazed further into him, her smiled faded, as if, in that moment, she could see just how twisted up he was about her.

He didn't turn away. Instead, he took one hand out of his pocket and held it out to her. His voice came out low and uncertain.

"Will you dance with me, Jackson?"

Her eyes flicked to his hand, and his heart pounded harder. If she said no, it would hurt like hell. He was dying to touch her, to have her sweet body pressed against his.

Cameron moved a little closer. "Whatever you want tonight, I'll do it better than anyone else."

Jackson closed her eyes. Maybe she was imagining the same things he was. Then her gaze met his and she nodded. "I already know that."

She lifted her soft hand, and his closed around it. If he had any say in this, he wasn't going to stop touching her for the rest of the night. They walked onto the dance floor, side by side, and Cameron stopped in the middle. The slow, sensual music filled the room. He turned to face her, their bodies so close to touching. He placed one of her hands on his shoulder, then the other, before slipping his arms around her and pulling her against him. In case there was still any question about what kind of dancing this would be.

Cameron looked down at her and raised an eyebrow. "You're...shorter tonight than you were yesterday."

"Why, Cameron, how sweet of you to say so," she said drily.

The corners of his mouth turned up. "There's more where that came from, Ms. McAllister."

She let out a little laugh, and he studied her for a moment. "Why wear high heels at all?" he asked. "They can't be comfortable."

"A small woman makes a man feel powerful," she said. "But a tall woman?"

Cameron chuckled. "I'm not touching that one."

"Fine," said Jackson. "You don't have to respond. But if I wear heels, I get more respect. Nothing makes a CEO listen like a woman who's taller than him."

Cameron nodded slowly, weighing her words. "Okay," he said. "I can see the logic. But it doesn't always work that way."

Jackson raised an eyebrow at him. "Really? You, the guy who hulks around growling at anyone who isn't doing what you want, you don't think size matters."

He smirked and leaned slowly toward her. "I never said size doesn't matter. But there are other things that can bring a man to his knees."

She gave him a bemused look, then rested her forehead on his arm. He moved his hands to the swell of her beautiful, round hips. And he pulled her even closer. Their bodies were flush, and her breasts pressed against his chest, spilling out like two delightful presents just for him.

This was heaven. Her body moved against his, and he responded. His hands traveled lower over her hips, every move playing out under his fingers. He buried his face in her hair and took a long, deep breath. And another. She sighed, and her body melted even closer. The word *more* echoed through him. Her hands moved up his shoulders and behind his neck, slowly weaving through his hair. He was more attracted to this woman than was wise. Maybe he didn't even care anymore. His heart pounded in his chest, begging him for more. Guests chatted, cameras flashed and glasses clinked around them, but everything was muted by this slow, sensual dance, with Jackson's body pressed against his.

The song ended, and they stopped. Jackson's eyelashes fluttered open, and her hands slipped from his neck. It was over. He let go of her, but neither of them moved apart. Her breasts rose and fell against him in short, erratic pants.

"One more night, Jackson."

She shuddered against him. He breathed in her scent again. His heart pounded harder, ready to explode, and thank God his suit coat hid the growing bulge in his pants. Was she going to turn him down, right here in the middle of the charity event dance floor?

"I'm not playing anymore, Jackson," he said in her ear. "This is real."

He straightened back up, and slowly she lifted her gaze to meet his. Her deep green eyes shone with heat and wonder.

"Yes, Cameron," she said. "One more night."

On the ride back to his building, he couldn't keep his hands off her. He was so far gone, and they hadn't even started. She laid her head against his chest, and her hand rested high on his thigh. Whatever she'd had around her shoulders had fallen away, revealing the low cut of her dress. He moved his hand in slow circles up and down her side, and she arched into his touch.

Tonight would never be enough. If she were his, if she stayed, he could wake up to her every morning, hold her every night and lose himself in everything she had to offer. Or whatever the hell she wanted. He could introduce her to all the dirty things she was curious about. And then some.

But Jackson wasn't his. She was flying back to New York tomorrow with no plans to return. And he couldn't get himself on a fucking airplane to save his life. Cameron gritted his teeth. He'd think about that problem later.

They pulled up in front of his building, and he helped her out into the warm night air. The car drove off and left them standing together under the starry sky. Jackson looked up at him, her eyes wide.

"What are we doing, Cameron?"

He chuckled. "Whatever you want to do."

Jackson smiled a little, but she glanced away. Damn. If she was talking about what they'd do once they got up to his bedroom, he could whisper a list of dirty ideas, just to see if she wanted to try one. The electricity that had sizzled between them for the last two weeks was threatening to spark out of control. Each time they gave in, it grew even more explosive between them. And neither of them was backing away. Yet he got the sense that wasn't what she was asking about.

His smile faded. "I don't know what the hell I'm doing."

Maybe that wasn't completely true. Back on the Opera House dance floor an idea had flickered to life inside him, and now he couldn't let go of it. *More.* He wanted more. So what if they lived on different continents. So what if they had only known each other for two weeks. Being with Jackson trumped every single obstacle he could see.

"I guess it doesn't matter," she said. "I'm leaving tomorrow." She blinked a couple times and gave him a tight smile that hit him straight in the gut.

He rested his hand on the smooth skin of her cheek. "All of this matters, Jackson."

No, he didn't feel like doing anything dirty at all. He just wanted her, plain and simple. He wanted to spend the night with his body over hers, her bright green eyes staring into his as they lost themselves in each other.

He looked at her for a long time, thinking everything he wanted to say. That this was so far past just getting each other off. That he was trying his hardest not to beg her to stay. That he wanted her to sleep in his bed every night so he could wake her up in creative ways every morning. How did he want all these things when they had never even spent a full night together? Maybe they would tonight.

She was watching him so intently, as if she were trying as hard as he was to figure out what mattered and why. He had to make tonight matter.

Cameron kissed her softly. "Let's go upstairs, sweetheart."

He took her hand and led her inside. He turned the key to the penthouse suite, and the elevator doors closed behind them. Jackson leaned against the back wall of the elevator, and he came up to her, covering her body with his. She tilted her hips against his hard length and he buried his face in her neck and inhaled. She smelled like heaven, some spicy, flowery shit that was driving him crazy. And then there was just Jackson, whose scent was now so imprinted on him that he'd probably still get hard twenty years from now if he found himself close enough to her.

"You know what I want?" he breathed.

She laughed. "I can guess."

"You're wrong."

She turned to him and raised her eyebrows. "What is it, then?"

He swallowed. "I want to make love to you so long and hard that you miss your plane tomorrow. And the next day. And the next."

There. He'd said it. Cameron watched her expression. Her gaze was soft and her mouth was parted, but she didn't say anything. Maybe that was a good thing.

"Stay the night, Jackson," he whispered. "Just to see what it's like."

Cameron's heart pounded, but he didn't move. She closed her eyes, and when they opened again, the dreamy look was gone. She wrinkled her brow. "I don't know. I—I didn't bring clothes. Or a toothbrush."

"I don't mind."

Was that a yes? If she stayed the night, he could show her what he had known that very first time in her hotel room. That this was different.

The elevator came to a stop, and the doors opened. He found her hand and squeezed it. She dropped her purse on the hall table and stopped. He came up behind her and rested his hands on the soft curve of her waist.

"Does this mean I'm going to see your bedroom tonight?" She smiled a slow, seductive smile that pushed away all thoughts of the future.

"Is that what you want?" he asked, pressing a kiss on her shoulder.

"Yes." She gave a sexy sigh.

"Good."

And Cameron needed to get there right about now. He dipped down and hooked his arm under her knees, lifting her up. Jackson sucked in a breath and laughed.

He carried her through the hall and set her down in the doorway. Jackson walked across the bedroom to the French doors that opened onto his balcony. The white walls twinkled with the harbor lights. Thank God his cleaning service had come the day before.

"It's beautiful here, Cameron," she said. "You're a really lucky man."

Cameron shoved his hands in his pockets. "I'm feeling pretty lucky right now, but it has nothing to do with my apartment."

She turned around and smiled a little. That dress was killing him. It was classy and sexy and showed off all the good parts. Which was basically everything. Jackson's smile grew wider.

"You know what I thought of when I put on this dress tonight?" she asked.

Cameron shook his head.

"I thought it might be a fun dress for a striptease."

She spoke these last words in her low, husky voice that gave a jolt to his already hardening cock. He nodded, not trusting his voice yet.

"You want to see me do that?" she asked softly.

"You have to ask?" He chuckled. "Hell, yes, I want you to strip for me."

Jackson bit her bottom lip. "I've never done anything like this. It might just look silly instead of sexy."

Cameron shook his head. "I'm going to find anything you do sexy, Jackson. You should know that by now." He let his gaze drift down her body. She had to know just how much he wanted her, no matter what she was doing. He met her eyes again and smiled. "If you can make me laugh when I'm this hard for you, all the better."

She licked her luscious lips and gestured to his bed. "There. Please."

Cameron took a few leisurely steps to the bed, slowing this game. He sat down on the edge and rested his forearms on his thighs. She slipped off her shoes and padded over to stand in front of him. He looked up at her.

"No touching," she whispered.

He smiled at her. "What about touching myself?"

Her eyes flared with a mix of surprise and heat.
"Oh," she murmured. Her eyes darted down between
his legs. "Yes. In fact, I want to see you make yourself
come while you're watching me."

"Oh, fuck," he muttered, squeezing his eyes shut as
his erection surged against the zipper of his pants. His
heart pumped hard against his chest. He was going to
come way too soon if he wasn't careful. "Just give me
a moment."

Cameron took a deep breath and stood up. He
brushed a kiss over her lips and moved past her, heading for his closet. He slipped off his jacket and unbuttoned his shirt, trying to calm himself down. This was
getting hotter by the minute, and they weren't even
touching yet. He walked back over to her and unfas-
tened his pants.

After spending the last two weeks hiding his interest in the office, he could drink her in slowly. This was
his own private fantasy world, tailored perfectly to the
two of them. He eased back onto the bed.

Her gaze dropped to the bulge in his pants, and she
smiled.

"Okay, here goes," she said.

She turned around and moved aside her hair. The
dress fastened behind her neck, and she fumbled with
the clasp for a moment before the two silky straps fell
over her shoulders. Cameron stared at the soft, bare
skin of her back. She looked over her shoulder, and her
smile was more seductive this time.

She turned around. Her hands still held the two

straps of her dress that had fallen over her shoulders and down her arms, revealing the tops of her breasts. She let the fabric fall a little farther until he could see the hint of her nipples.

All night she hadn't been wearing a bra.

Cameron reached into his pants and took himself in his hand. Jackson's gaze followed his hand, and her eyes widened. He eased down his pants and let his erection free. His tip was already wet, and he rubbed his palm over it.

"Keep going, sweetheart," he said.

Her eyes darted back up to his, and he drank in all her want, the need that he hoped went beyond physical satisfaction.

Jackson slipped her thumbs under the satiny black fabric and rubbed her nipples in slow circles. Her breath caught, and she teased harder. Cameron gave himself a couple rough strokes and moaned. She let the straps fall so the dress hung at her waist, revealing the most beautiful breasts. His mouth watered as he imagined taking one in his mouth and playing with the other. There were so many things he wanted to do with her nipples, much dirtier. His hand moved faster as pleasure rushed through him. She took her breasts in her hands and squeezed, and his cock throbbed hard in his grip.

"I'm close," he ground out.

"Good."

She teased her nipples and watched him get himself off for another few beats. Then she turned in profile and found a zipper hidden on the side of her dress.

Slowly, she pulled it down, revealing more and more of that creamy skin. He was going to come any second now. She shifted her hips and guided the silky material down her thighs to the floor. All that was left was a pair of lacy red panties. He swallowed hard, fighting against the building surge.

Jackson stepped out of the dress and within his reach. She watched over her shoulder as she slipped her fingers into those lacy panties. Just as she bent over to lower them, her gaze opened into something raw and vulnerable.

Everything exploded in a frenzy of euphoric bursts. He kept his gaze fixed on Jackson, her eyes wide, as he let out a torn cry and emptied himself into his hand and onto his stomach. His whole body contracted, and he growled out her name.

Seconds passed. Or maybe minutes. Cameron tried to kick his mind back into gear.

Jackson stepped forward and caressed the back of his neck. "That was really..." she faltered. "Thanks for playing out this little scene of mine."

He hung his head. It was incredible. He had seen other women strip before, and none of them had gotten him going like this. Not even close. But this was probably the wrong time to bring up other naked women.

How could he make her understand? Just carrying out their fantasies wasn't what made this little strip show good. She was the one who brought this beyond teenage jack-off dreams into something much more for him.

He had this one last night to show her. And he wasn't going to screw it up.

Cameron looked up at her. Jackson was naked, and he was a mess.

He kissed the swell of her hips. "Shower?"

She smiled a little. "Sure."

She followed him into the bathroom and leaned against the counter. She was biting her lower lip again.

"You okay?" he asked.

She nodded. "More than okay. I just didn't realize sex could be like this." She chuckled. "I'm not sure I can go back to a regular relationship."

What the hell?

Cameron crossed his arms over his chest. "You think good sex and exploring what turns you on don't go together with a regular relationship?"

Jackson shrugged. "I don't know. I've had a few relationships, and I certainly never had sex like this. Not even close."

"And you've developed a theory based on those assholes?"

She pursed her lips.

"In my experience, guys either want sexy or they want a relationship. I've never been the sexy type." She glanced away. "After my last boyfriend cheated on me, it made me wonder. So here we are. I get to see what it's like to be the sexy type instead."

He raised an eyebrow. "You like it?"

Jackson smirked. "Definitely has its advantages."

Steam came from the shower, and Cameron felt the

water with his hand. He stepped in and motioned for her to join him. Jackson entered the shower, her body skimming against his.

"Keep going," he said, running his hands over her bare shoulders. "I'm curious to hear your theories on what men want."

"You don't agree? Men want to have lots of sex with a certain kind of woman. Then they settle down with another kind of woman." She tilted her head. "The reason I'm here is because of your reputation with that first kind of woman, right?"

"What my reputation is and what I want are two different things."

"You don't want to pick up women in hotel bars for sex?"

Cameron sighed. "You want to hear what I think men want?"

Jackson swallowed. "I'm not sure, but go ahead."

"I think men want a lot of hot sex, and if it's in a relationship, all the better. But that's hard to find. So some men go for the relationship and compromise on the sex." He tucked her long damp hair behind her ear and caressed her cheek. "And other men go for the sex, knowing something is missing. Hoping that at some point he meets a woman who can show him what that *something* is."

He found her mouth, wet and warm, and he kissed her. He ran his hands down the curve of her waist and up again, and he nuzzled her cheek with his chin.

"Maybe that second kind of man doesn't even know

that's what he's looking for until he finds it," he whispered. "But once he finds it, he doesn't want to go back."

She stilled, and her expression was unreadable. But there was one little tell that gave him hope that she was just as twisted up about this as he was. His hand stopped over the furious pulse at the base of her neck.

The familiar desire for her was returning, but he wasn't giving in to it yet. Losing himself inside her wasn't enough. He wanted something beyond that tonight.

He didn't move. "What do you think about my theory?"

"I'll have to think about it," she said. "Now I'd like to wash you. Slowly."

Her mouth curved into a lazy, seductive grin. She reached for the soap and rubbed it between her hands under the water. She set it back on the shelf and began with his shoulders. In slow circles, she washed his arms, her soft fingers gliding over his skin. Her eyes had a look of wonder in them as she traced the lines of muscle and trails of hair. How these things held her attention was a mystery when she had her own gloriously curvy body, but he wasn't going to point that out right now.

She turned for more soap and worked her way down, across his chest and over the tense muscles of his stomach. And lower.

Heaven. He was in heaven.

He grabbed on to the shower wall to steady himself. She circled closer as he grew harder. She gave his cock a few sudsy strokes, and he tipped his head back and groaned.

All his frustrations and self-recriminations from the night were gone. The water ran down her arms and over her magnificent breasts.

Cameron swallowed hard. "My turn."

He soaped up his hands and smiled. He started at her feet and worked his way up the swell of her thighs and hips, around her beautiful rear and narrow midriff. And her breasts. Goddamn, he was obsessed. He tore his eyes away. But after a few sweeps of her smooth arms, he was done with the washing. He closed his eyes and rested his forehead on hers. He let his fingers glide over her back, her waist, memorizing each curve, as they stood under the faucet. She rested her head on his chest, and he closed his arms around her. "Let me take you to bed, Jackson."

He turned off the shower, grabbed a towel and wrapped her in it. After drying himself off a bit, he took her hand. "Ready?"

She didn't move. She looked up at him hesitantly. "There's a lot of things we haven't tried yet."

She wanted to play again, and his dick didn't miss the message. But he wanted more than just playing around.

He shook his head. "Not tonight."

"Tonight is all we have." Her eyes seemed to glaze over, like she was already halfway through her fantasy. Which he was not giving in to.

Cameron put his hand on her cheek. "You miss your plane tomorrow and stay with me, and we'll try whatever you want. We'll try things you've never even thought of." He brushed his lips over hers. "But not tonight. If this is our last night, we're done with fantasies. I told you before. This is real."

Her eyes widened. The creases still lined her forehead, but he waited her out.

Finally she nodded. "Okay." She walked over to the bed and sat down primly on the edge. Her wet hair dripped down her body, and she shook it behind her shoulders. "So, what do we do?"

Cameron laughed. "You've never had vanilla sex?"

Jackson rolled her eyes. "Until two weeks ago, that's all I'd ever had. After I leave this apartment, it's probably all I'll do for the rest of my life."

Cameron sat down next to her on the bed. Their bodies brushed against each other's, but he didn't touch her. He inhaled deeply and exhaled slowly. Here lay the biggest problem. She still thought what she felt was about sex. Because she was trying things she had never tried. But he had played more than his share of dirty games before. He had played enough to know that no game was enough to make him feel like he did on the Opera House dance floor with Jackson in his arms. And he had felt that with all of his clothes on.

But he couldn't explain that. He had to show her instead.

Cameron leaned over and traced Jackson's wet hair down her back. "I think vanilla could be just as good as any game if we do it right."

"Is that so?" Her voice was soft and dreamy.

"Let's find out." He nodded to the pillows. "Come lie down with me."

He lay on his side, and she settled against him. She looked at him expectantly, as if she had no idea what to do next. Maybe she didn't. And maybe he didn't know what he was getting into, either.

Cameron found her hand. Was it trembling? He brought it to his mouth for a soft kiss and placed it on his waist. He cupped her cheek with his hand and kissed the corner of her mouth, then her bottom lip. He slid his hand down her shoulder and back up behind her neck as he opened his mouth and found her tongue. Her fingers tightened around his waist, so he did it again. She pulled him against her and rocked her hips. He twitched and ached, and she rocked again. Her round breasts pressed against his chest, and he cupped one with his hand, squeezing as he deepened the kiss. She moaned and sighed, moving against him, setting his body on fire.

He rolled her over onto her back, spreading her legs with his knees. He settled onto his elbows and caught her gaze. And held it. His mind reeled through all the things he couldn't say. That this had somehow become more than just a complicated mistake. That he was starting to think his own ten-year plan included her. That he couldn't imagine a life where he never did this again.

And then she moved. All thoughts disappeared except one. Jackson. Cameron couldn't hold it together any longer. He ran his length over every wet, delicious fold. Her eyes grew hazy with pleasure, but she didn't look away. It was incredible. This time he wasn't going to bury his head between her legs or tease her ass or do any of the other nasty, hot shit to make her come. This time, it was just the two of them, face-to-face. And if she could just see what he was feeling right now, everything might turn out right.

He glided along her slippery core and restrained the urge to move faster. He wasn't going to come on her stomach, no matter how good it would be. She widened her legs, opening herself to him, and she tilted her hips, meeting each of his movements. Her breaths got shorter and louder, and she chanted his name, how good he felt, how big he was.

Something inside him was about to explode.

"Now, Cameron." She gasped, her eyelids fluttering. "I want you now."

He stilled. "You can have me anytime you want, Jackson," he breathed. "Anytime."

He pushed back and grabbed a condom from inside his nightstand. He rolled it on as she watched, her mouth parted. She was so beautiful. He had to make her see just how right they were together. If he could get this one last night together right, maybe she would stay a little longer.

He pressed his tip at her entrance and slipped his arms under her shoulders.

"Yes, Cameron," she whispered, moving her hips.

He buried his head in the warm, lush scent of her neck and, slowly, he pushed in. At her sounds of pleasure, he pushed deeper and deeper. Finally, he was buried inside her. And he could have stayed there forever, on the edge of infinite bliss. But Jackson wanted more.

So he gave her one hard thrust, and she cried out.

"Vanilla feels good to me right now." He caught her earlobe between his teeth. "What do you think?"

"Yes." She sighed. He gave her another unyielding thrust. "Yes. Yes."

He moved inside her, setting a slow, relentless pace. She matched his rhythm, urging him on faster, harder. *Yes, yes.* Her voice echoed inside him, over and over. Cameron bit his tongue, distracting himself from the urge to come. He held her face in his hands and looked down at her, giving her everything.

"I'm so close, Cameron," she whispered.

He reached between them and found her clit. Her mouth fell open and he swirled his fingers firmer. She clawed at his back as he drove into her steadily. Her body shook and clenched under him as she fell apart in his arms, calling his name.

"Oh, God, Cameron. Yes."

At the sound of his name, his whole body exploded. He came in long spasms, emptying inside her. He held her tightly as his hips moved against hers, over and over in the most primitive urge to drive himself deeper, deeper inside her forever.

Jackson melted under him, her gaze dreamy and unfocused. It was them, together, that made her look that way. Did she understand that now?

She stroked his arm, pressing her fingers against his muscles.

"You're amazing," Jackson whispered. "I still can't get over it, and I don't think I ever will."

She used the word *will*. Did she imagine a scenario where they were together?

Cameron smiled. "You really know how to make a man feel good." He wove his hand into her damp hair. "Just the way you're looking at me right now. I feel like my heart's going to burst."

The corners of her mouth turned up, slowly spreading into a smile. She looked genuinely surprised. "You know, you're good at keeping these kinds of things to yourself. I can never read you."

He blinked down at her, registering her comment. Did she not understand that he was affected, too? He tried for the best answer he could come up with.

"Actions speak louder than words, right?"

Jackson laughed. "Are we talking about actions in bed?"

"Yes, we are." He bent down and brushed his lips against her. "You need me to spell it out for you?"

She nodded. "Humor me."

He pulled out and rolled out of bed to throw away the condom. She didn't move, but she followed him with her eyes. He slid back over her, resting on his elbows.

He brushed his thumb along her bottom lip. "This is good between us. Really good. And not just in bed. So don't go. Stay here in Sydney with me."

She puffed out a breath and looked away. "Even if I wanted to stay, I have to go back. I have a job and an apartment. And a ten-year plan."

Cameron's heart gave a surge. Not the answer he was looking for, but maybe there was hope. She had thought this through. Which meant maybe she had considered staying.

"A plan to quit your job and travel?" he asked.

"I just want to explore a little," she said. "Travel and work in new places, that kind of thing. But first I need to get myself on better financial footing, pay off my student loans. Someday."

He raised an eyebrow. She gave him a wry smile.

"Good things come to those who wait, right?" she added. "My mother's philosophy."

"Did it work for her?"

Jackson snorted. "Not really. Which is why she wants me to firm up my plans."

"How much money do these plans involve?"

"I'm still working that part out." Jackson frowned.

"Maybe you've waited long enough, Jackson," he said slowly. "Maybe it's time to stop waiting and start doing the things you really want to do."

She wrinkled her nose. "Give up my hard-won apartment and my job to travel until the money ran out?"

"I'd give you a job," he said.

Jackson laughed. "Was that an interview the other day in your office?"

"If you want it to be." He leaned down to kiss her neck. "But I'd hire you even without the extra services."

"Good to know."

He cupped her face in his hands so she was looking at him. "I'm serious, Jackson."

She blinked at him, and for a moment her eyes welled up.

"I can't just abandon my life in New York. Not right now, when my only Plan B involves moving back in with my mother." She shuddered. "Maybe I'll come back sometime and visit. When I can afford to take some time off."

He shook his head slowly. "Not good enough."

"Just pick up and go? That is what my mother would call completely unrealistic thinking." She brushed her fingers over his jaw. "I have monthly payments and no real savings. I'd be completely dependent on you."

Cameron shook his head. "It doesn't have to be that way."

She was silent for a while, her fingers lingering on his jaw. "Maybe you could come to New York instead."

He froze. He should have prepared for this question, but he hadn't. The board must have mentioned that he never traveled. Cameron closed his eyes.

"I can't," he said flatly. He tamped down the panic that came from even thinking about that last time. Cameron took a deep breath. "Look, even if I wanted to, I wouldn't make it there. When I flew here to Sydney, I went a little crazy. If Simon hadn't been there to talk me down, I would have been led off in handcuffs."

"Oh. I'm sorry," she whispered. But there wasn't a hint of pity in her voice. A crease formed between her eyebrows. "Is that why you don't go to board meetings?"

Cameron sighed. "Partly. But the other reason is true, too. I'd rather not be in the same room as my father."

"But the no-flying thing isn't public, right?" she said quietly.

He gave her a tight smile. "Bad for business."

So there it was. He had laid it all out for her and gotten his answer. She wasn't staying in Sydney, and he was too messed up to be able to follow her back.

Her fingers moved to his neck, and she played with his hair.

"What happened? I mean, what made you lose it?" she asked. Then she shook her head. "Never mind. You don't have to talk about it."

But she deserved to know. Cameron rolled on his back and looked up at the ceiling. "On our last mission, the plane was hit. Some of us got out, but others?" He shook his head. "Every time I think about flying, I flash to those seconds when the plane crashed into the ground. The other side went down first and killed the two guys closest to the rear. I was sitting on the other side, watching… Why the hell did I make it and not those guys? One of them was married with a kid and another on the way. His family needed him. I was a young, cocky shit, and I didn't need to live. But I did."

Jackson slowed her movements. "I'm glad you did. Really glad."

Those words felt good. He glanced down at her and frowned. "Just about everyone who goes to war has a story like that. It's nothing special."

"That doesn't make it easier," she whispered. She propped herself up on her arm. Her soft breaths tickled his chest, and he couldn't stop thinking about how warm and perfect her body was against his. It made everything just a little better. And her soft, husky voice was already getting him hard again.

Cameron reached out to find her hand, and he laced his fingers in hers.

She leaned forward for another soft kiss. "If this really is our last night, let's make it good."

CHAPTER FOURTEEN

JACKSON SANK INTO an airport security seat and slipped her shoes back on. She hadn't gotten much sleep the night before, and her mind didn't seem to be functioning properly. Questions like *Why the hell did you walk out of Cameron's apartment this morning?* and *When did you get to be such a mess over a man?* had been running through her mind for hours.

She wasn't really considering quitting her job in New York for more time with Cameron, was she? Cameron, the man who wouldn't fly. Goodbye, ten-year plan. Goodbye, dreams of travel and adventure. No, she couldn't do that.

The ache of leaving him would fade at some point, wouldn't it? Because this was unbearable. She had turned him down when he'd offered to take her to the airport. Out of sight, out of mind. Now, only a few hours after she had last buried her face in his chest and breathed in his warm, musky scent, she already regretted it. A few more minutes with his arms around her in the back of the car wouldn't have made this moment better, but it would be one more memory. And in their two-week history, that was something.

But maybe it was better like this. Most of their morning had been without clothes, and it was hard to think about much of anything when Cameron wasn't dressed. But if he had come back to her hotel room when she'd packed, she would have probably forgotten half her belongings. If she had spent the ride to the airport against his warm, hard body, she might have begged him...

But begged for what? For Cameron to come with her? He had already made it clear that he didn't do airplanes.

So what if staying here in Sydney with him would mean crossing off pages of entries in her little red book. So what if he introduced her to games that were made for porn movies. Really good porn movies. She had wanted to travel for her whole life. She wasn't giving up her little red book or her ten-year plan for a guy she had met two weeks ago. And that was that.

Jackson blew out a breath and looked at her watch. She still had another hour before her plane took off. She stood up and grabbed her carry-on bag. Coffee usually made everything a little better. Maybe it would even work for heartbreak. Not that this was heartbreak. It was just...readjustment.

The nearest café had a line to the door, but Jackson didn't have anything better to do. She rolled her bag over to the little shop and parked herself behind the last person. And tried not to look at her phone. She had already looked at Cameron's message about a hundred times. He wasn't going to send another one unless she responded. Which she wasn't going to. At least not until she was far away.

Jackson rubbed her eyes and looked for a distraction. She grabbed a paper off the newsstand and scanned the front page, slowing to a stop when she reached the bottom. There, in full color, was a photo of two A-list actors posing on the dance floor of the Bennelong Room at the Sydney Opera House. But it wasn't the actors who caught her eye. It was the little black dress in the background.

Her little black dress. And Cameron's large, sensual hands in the middle of her rear. His face was lowered to hers. The photo hadn't caught either of them directly, but it was enough.

She remembered that moment. He was already half-hard and had whispered words in her ear that had made her forget they were in a public place. And she had brushed a lock of hair off his face, as if he were hers for real.

She stared down at the photo as she raced to spin this most public breach of conduct. Technically, they were off the clock at that point, but the board probably wouldn't care. Could they just make some claim about helping her blend in? Besides, her face was turned, so maybe she wasn't so identifiable. Damn. She was in PR, for God's sake. She could do better than that, couldn't she?

Except she couldn't. All she could think about right now was the look on Cameron's face. It was a combination of want and longing and something else she didn't

even know how to process. And it was printed on the
front of the *Sydney Morning Herald* for everyone to see.

Maybe the Blackmore Inc. board didn't read the *Sydney Morning Herald*.

Jackson refolded the paper and slid it back into the
newsstand, photo side down.

Shit.

She couldn't even pretend this was a mistake. She
had known the risks, and that hadn't stopped her. Because in the end she didn't want to stop. This time,
she'd wanted to give in. And she couldn't make herself regret it.

What the hell was she going to do? Maybe her brain
would kick back into gear somewhere over the Pacific.
Because she had forty-eight hours before she'd be standing in front of the board. And Harlan Blackmore. If she
didn't come up with something, Harlan Blackmore and
his board would come up with their own explanations.
And none of them would be good.

Even the magical powers of coffee couldn't help
make this disaster better.

Just as she squeezed her eyes shut in a futile attempt
to make it all go away, her phone rang. She pulled it
out of her bag, the word *Mom* in large letters across
the screen.

"This isn't such a great time, Mom," she said.

"Oh, honey, you're always too busy," her mother said.
"How do you expect to keep a good man if you don't
even have time for your mother?"

What was Jackson expecting? Anything in the range

of *What's wrong, honey?* was a stretch, of course, but maybe just *I'll try you later*?

"My plane is boarding soon," Jackson said. Soon, as in within the next forty-five minutes. "Was there something quick you wanted to say?"

That got her attention. "Oh, no. Am I calling internationally? Heavens." Her mother let out a long breath. "Well, I just wanted to remind you that Marcello and Marco are turning three in a few weeks. I didn't want you to forget. You know, some single dads are coming, some who might consider—"

"Thanks, Mom. I'll be there," she said. "Look, I have to go."

Jackson stuffed her phone back into her bag. Her career was teetering on the edge of disaster, her whole body ached for Cameron and her mother was trying to fix her up with single dads. Welcome home.

Jackson smoothed her dark blue skirt and checked to make sure the top button of her blouse was still buttoned. She had dressed in her most conservative suit, but it wasn't helping. She was the woman who they had sent over to tame Harlan Blackmore's rebellious son, only to fall headfirst for his charms. And land on the front page of the *Sydney Morning Herald*. Which maybe, by some miracle, the board hadn't seen.

She wasn't the woman they thought they'd hired. She wasn't the woman *she* thought they'd hired, either.

"I'm Jackson McAllister, to see the board," she announced to the receptionist.

The woman gave her a once-over and raised her eyebrows. "Right this way, Ms. McAllister."

Jackson followed the receptionist down the hall, ignoring the top-floor view of New York City. It was hard to believe that she had walked down this same hall less than three weeks ago. The person she was the last time she met the board felt far, far away. Her fling with Cameron was stupid and unprofessional. She had known it at the time, and she had still gone back to him, again and again. It was exactly the kind of mistake Jackson thought she wasn't capable of making. The board must have thought the same, since they'd sent her over there, despite Cameron's reputation.

Now she had to hope that none of them happened to scan the front page of the Sydney newspaper two days ago. If she could just get through this meeting and close the file with Blackmore Inc., she could catch her breath. And try to figure out what the hell she was doing.

The receptionist opened the door to a large conference room at the end of the hall. The first slide of her presentation was already displayed on the wide screen across the room. Harlan Blackmore sat at the head of a long table, and the board members took up the seats along the two sides. The only empty seat was at the other end, nearest the door. She walked to her place, pulled out the chair and froze. On the table in front of her was the *Sydney Morning Herald* from two days before. Her own little black dress was no less recognizable, nor were Cameron's strategically placed hands.

Cameron. Just this little glimpse of him brought on

a wash of want and longing she had tried so hard to put behind her these last forty-eight hours.

Don't go. Stay here in Sydney with me. He had held her face and kissed her until all doubts were gone. But the next morning she had left. And now she was here in New York, across the conference table from his father, about to discuss the specifics of her last two weeks. Shit.

Jackson swallowed hard and straightened up. At least her first question was answered. They knew. She had played out this scenario in her head, but how did she decide to spin it? Her mind had gone blank.

So she sat down, folded the paper back up and set it aside.

"You have my report, but—" she gestured to the newspaper next to her "—it seems you want to discuss something else."

A smile formed on Harlan Blackmore's hard countenance, but it held no warmth. "I already knew my son would go to all lengths to tell me to fuck off. I just assumed you were too smart for that. Apparently, I was wrong. But who knows how a woman's mind works."

Jackson pressed her lips together, shutting down various hotheaded responses that came to mind. She didn't even know where to start being offended. At the insult to her intelligence? At the insult to women in general? Or should she be offended that not one of the board members spoke up?

"What can I say?" Blackmore's voice held a hint of admiration. "He's my son. He's good at what he does."

He took a single sheet of paper from in front of him

and passed it down the table. Each man glanced down at it before passing it on. Harlan Blackmore was putting on a show, reminding her of who ran this meeting.

The paper landed in front of her. Jackson clenched her jaw and forced herself to look down. It was a printout of an email from Cameron to the other three members on his team, written on the first day she had been at the Blackmore Inc. office. It was short, and one of the sentences was highlighted in yellow, doubtlessly by Blackmore himself, just to make sure no one missed the message: *Figure out Jackson McAllister's weak spots at dinner tonight. Tomorrow we'll discuss how to exploit them.*

Jackson could feel the heat creeping up her neck as she reread the sentence. No. This couldn't have come from the man who'd asked her to stay yesterday. It just couldn't.

Except that everything else about it looked real. Surely it was below even Harlan Blackmore to fake something like this. And what would he gain by doing it? But if it wasn't faked, then Cameron took her back to his apartment just to discredit her.

He wouldn't do that, would he?

"Ms. McAllister?" Harlan Blackmore's voice boomed from the other end of the table.

Shit. She was still at the beginning of this meeting from hell, with no escape in sight. Yes, she could get through this. She had been through worse. But what this meant about her last two weeks with Cameron stung more than she wanted it to.

Jackson took a deep breath and met Harlan Blackmore's cool gaze. "You have an email that says your son will discredit me, and you have a news photo of him fondling me. It's my job to worry about what these items say about your son, not about me. We can start that discussion by looking over my report."

The board members were watching this discussion play out, tennis-match style. Their heads turned together for Blackmore's response. Except nothing came. His expression didn't falter, but the hesitation itself was all the answer she needed.

The corners of his mouth turned up in what could have been amusement. "I can see why he went for you."

"I'll take that as a compliment," said Jackson with a tight smile. "Shall we begin?"

Jackson settled into her seat and leaned over to pull her files out of her bag. But as she reached in, the conference room door handle clicked, and the receptionist's clipped tones came through the doorway.

"...in the middle of a meeting, but—"

"Thank you for escorting me. I'm here for the board meeting, too."

His voice. No. Impossible.

She sat up straight and slowly turned toward the door. Cameron was taking up most of the doorway, dressed in jeans and a black T-shirt, carrying a leather jacket. He had grown a beard again or forgotten to shave. More likely the latter, considering the messy hair and dark circles under his eyes. Those deep blue eyes were a little glazed over, but they were alive with emotion. And he was staring right at her.

"What?" she whispered. "What are you doing here?"

Cameron had the nerve to chuckle. "I came to help you through this. Though by the look on my father's face, I'm guessing you're doing just fine on your own."

Jackson's heart raced faster, and her fingers tingled. Somehow, he had made it here. The man who had sworn off planes forever had flown here, to New York. She ached to touch him, to make sure he was real. She ached to do a lot more than that. So she grabbed the file in front of her and held on tight.

Because...that email. He had planned to discredit her. He had written it out and sent it to his team. Had he come to New York to play her, start off nice before he finished her off? She didn't want to believe that the Cameron she knew would do that, but he was the son of Harlan Blackmore. Good at what he did. And he had shown her just how much he loved playing games. And winning them.

But Jackson wasn't going to think about that. She sat on the edge of her chair, searching for something to say. Harlan Blackmore beat her to it.

"Well, son, this is a surprise," he rumbled. "If I had known that pussy would bring you to a board meeting, I would have arranged for it long ago."

Jackson sucked in a harsh breath, and Cameron froze. His hands balled into fists, and his jaw worked angrily. This was bad in so many ways. Harlan Blackmore was just as awful as Cameron had insinuated.

Even worse. And Cameron looked about two seconds away from punching his father in the face.

"Don't, Cameron," she said. "What's the point?"

Her voice shook a little, but she was beyond caring.

Cameron closed his eyes and let out a long breath. He unclenched his hands, and his heavy shoulders came down a fraction of an inch.

"I would have thought a comment like that was beneath even you, Father," he said slowly. "But you're full of surprises, as well."

He headed for the corner of the room and grabbed an extra chair. He set it down next to Jackson. What the hell was he doing? She couldn't sit next to him. She couldn't listen to his smooth, deep voice and smell his musky scent and not react.

She took a steadying breath. It didn't work.

Cameron was watching her. Waiting. She couldn't do this. She glanced over at him, but he was looking down at the printout of his email. And frowning.

Slowly, he met her gaze again. He didn't reject the paper or call it out as a fake.

"Later," he said softly. But his eyes said more. *You know me.*

Jackson swallowed hard. Did she?

But they were in a meeting. Her voice was going to shake if she spoke again. Which would only feed Harlan Blackmore's attacks. Cameron was still waiting for her to begin. He thought she could do this. And she still couldn't get her mind back into gear.

Finally, Cameron leaned back in his chair and looked

out at the board. "Ms. McAllister spent the last two weeks boosting the Blackmore Inc. image, and the write-ups we've gotten are evidence of her success. So I'm ready to listen to her plan for our next steps."

Right. Just talk about the plans. Don't think about anything else.

So she pulled out her file, cleared her throat and started to speak.

CHAPTER FIFTEEN

CAMERON HADN'T MOVED a muscle for the last thirty minutes. Jackson's presentation was full of angles he hadn't even considered. She had dropped hints about her ideas during her stay in Sydney, but she hadn't asked for his approval. She had managed a perfect balance between respecting his freedom when it came to running his business but answering first and foremost to the board. The woman was amazing.

But he already knew that. What he hadn't counted on was her ability to take control of the meeting and steer it right back on her course. She had completely and unapologetically shut down the discussion of the front-page appearance of their less-than-professional dance. Even his father looked impressed. And that was saying something.

"That's my proposal for future actions," concluded Jackson. She turned off the projector and returned to her seat. "Any questions?"

Harlan Blackmore leaned back in his chair and laced

his fingers together. "So you're proposing that we hire a Sydney-based firm for ongoing strategy?"

Jackson shook her head. "No, Mr. Blackmore. I'm suggesting *your son* hires a Sydney-based firm. This is an ongoing project that Cameron needs to be a part of if we're looking for success." She turned to the rest of the board. "The virtual conferencing system I'm recommending is standard in most companies now, and it will allow for regular updates from the Sydney office."

The room was silent. Jackson had just proposed a giant step toward getting him out from under his father's thumb. And not just in the PR department. He'd rejected the idea of a virtual conferencing system before, thinking his father would abuse it. All this time he'd thought distancing the Sydney branch was the best way to keep the board from meddling. But from the way Jackson had presented it just now, this tool would give him his independence; it would ensure that decisions regarding the Sydney office weren't made in his absence. And Jackson had carefully presented her recommendations in a way that sidestepped Harlan Blackmore.

"So, Ms. McAllister, you're writing yourself out of this plan?" his father asked. "What will your firm say about that?"

Cameron clenched his fists. His father hadn't missed any of the subtleties of Jackson's plan. The board had assigned her the task of boosting the company's image and getting his errant son under control, and she had come back with a plan that gave that same son more power. Which meant Harlan Blackmore had less. He was too savvy to outwardly dismiss Jackson's plan, but he wasn't above looking for ways to put her at a disadvantage.

But Harlan Blackmore wasn't the first CEO Jackson had met. She raised an eyebrow at him. "My job is to recommend the best plan of action for your company, not ours. My success record speaks for itself. That's why I was assigned this account in the first place."

The room grew quiet again. Finally, one of the board members leaned forward and picked up the sheet of recommendations Jackson had passed out.

"This is a really solid plan." He looked down at Cameron. "But some of this depends on whether you want this role, Mr. Blackmore."

Cameron nodded. "After I've taken a little time off, I'll be ready."

"I'm in favor, as well," said another member.

"Should we take it to a vote?"

Cameron blinked. Maybe the board wasn't completely under his father's command. Maybe showing up at this meeting was enough to get them to listen. And Jackson had just created a way for him to do it. One that didn't require flying or being in the same room as his father.

Yep. He was definitely in love with her.

The vote passed, and they adjourned. He hung back as one of the board members shook Jackson's hand. He couldn't stop himself from staring. But the hard clap on his shoulder jolted him back to reality.

"You flew all the way here for this meeting, son."

Cameron flinched at the word *son*. There was no escaping it. He was Harlan Blackmore's son, not just Harlan Senior's grandson. But he had a choice in how he lived that out.

He cleared his face of emotion and turned to his father. "It was important, so I came."

His father scowled. "You're making a mistake if you let a woman like that make decisions for you."

Cameron smiled. "You're in a room full of people who disagree."

His father was quiet.

"How long will you be in New York?" he finally asked.

Cameron took a deep breath. "Not sure yet."

"Come by the office again," said his father.

"I'll think about it."

Cameron shook his father's hand, and his father left. Slowly, the board members trickled out until it was just Jackson and him left. She looked at him carefully.

"You heading out?" he asked softly.

She nodded. She gathered her belongings with the delicate hands he had dreamed about last night, and they headed for the elevator.

The tension between them crackled. Every move she made echoed in his body, as he waited for that first touch. She was all buttoned up in that suit, and her hair was twisted into a tight bun like she was waiting for someone to take it down.

Please let it be me.

The elevator doors opened, and she stepped in and pushed the button. She didn't look at him until the doors closed.

"I thought you didn't fly."

He crossed his arms. "Until yesterday I didn't."

"And then you suddenly got over your fear?" She raised an eyebrow.

"Not quite," he said. "The real story involves a shitty day on my part when you left, enough tranquilizers to subdue a horse and a really big favor by Simon."

Her eyes softened. "He came with you? You told me he was never coming back to the US again."

"He wasn't. As I said, it was a really big favor."

"Oh." She looked down at the floor.

He frowned. It was the second flight Simon had coached him through, and Cameron hoped to God that it was the last time he ever had to ask for a favor like that again. He hoped that the next time he had to force himself onto a plane, Jackson would be sitting next to him instead. He shuddered. Just thinking about climbing into that metal coffin was going to flip the switch back into that awful abyss. And he wasn't going back there. Not now. Not if he didn't have to.

After descending a few more floors, she turned to him again. "Why are you here?"

He blinked. Did she really not understand?

"I'm here for you," he said slowly. "Because your career is at stake while the board just thinks Harlan Blackmore's stubborn son is acting up again. And if you got fired and I just got a new PR plan, then…"

She looked up at him, eyes wide. He couldn't stop himself this time. They were still in the elevator of his father's building, where they were probably being watched by someone, but he couldn't wait any longer. He turned to her and ran the backs of his fingers down her cheek.

"Then none of this could work out right," he whispered.

The elevator dinged, and the doors opened into the lobby. Their shoes echoed as they crossed the stone floor, but she didn't say a word. They walked out into the November wind. Damn, it was cold. Why the hell did anyone live in this climate? Cameron put on his jacket and zipped it up, then he looked down at Jackson. She had some sexy little pair of shoes on, and she was already shivering.

"Can we find somewhere to talk?" he asked. "Somewhere a little warmer?"

She studied him. "I don't know. I really appreciate that you came all this way to help me out today, especially considering you never fly. But spending time together is only going to make the goodbye harder." She blinked up at him, and for a moment, she looked young and vulnerable. This was the same woman who could handle Harlan Blackmore and his board. But the way she was staring up at him, so lost and worried, he wanted to hold her and make her smile again. He was so gone on this woman.

He gently interlaced her cold fingers in his. "Jackson, let's get a taxi and go somewhere far from here. Somewhere warm. Then you can spend all the time you want telling me why we shouldn't do this."

She smiled, and some of the lost look faded. Finally, she whispered, "Okay."

The taxi ride was quiet, and the car dropped them off in front of an old-fashioned Italian café. He held the door open for her, and the warm air flooded out. The place was nearly empty. Jackson sat down at one of the tiny tables by the window. She crossed her legs and rubbed her hands together. God, she looked cold. She belonged in Sydney with him. But they were a long way from that.

The waitress came up to take their orders, but Cameron had no idea what the hell he was supposed to order in a place like this. There were all sorts of girly-looking breads and desserts, but he wasn't hungry. Jackson was the only thing on his mind right now.

Thankfully, she just ordered a coffee. He did, too, and the waitress disappeared, leaving them in silence.

"Where's Simon?" she asked after a while.

"Miami."

Her eyebrows rose. She waited for more, but he wasn't going to get into that.

Simon hadn't said a word about his plans, but Cameron knew what he was doing. If Simon had flown to Miami, he was going to the house of the woman he'd never got over. Who he thought he never deserved in the first place. Who was now married. Even moving halfway around the world hadn't helped that wound heal. But that was Simon's shit to tell, not his.

Besides, he hadn't come here to talk about Simon. It was time to clear the air. "First, about that email my father showed you. I wrote it the morning before we met." Cameron added, "Before we met in the office. As soon as I saw who you were, I called that off."

She looked at him for a while, and a little of the hurt in her eyes disappeared. But not all of it.

"You were amazing today, Jackson," he whispered.

She gave him a wry smile. "I didn't get fired today." Her smile faded. "But the board found out about us. I felt unprofessional. And cheap."

"My father's such an asshole," Cameron muttered, hanging his head and closing his eyes. "You're not cheap, Jackson. So, so far from that." He rubbed the back of his neck.

"Besides," he added, "the reason I picked you up that night at the hotel was because I found out the board was sending someone over to get me in line. So I did the opposite. How's that for unprofessional?" He looked up at her again. A strand of hair had escaped her bun, and she tucked it behind her ear. Damn, she was beautiful. "Well, maybe that wasn't the only reason. You also looked sexy as hell."

She laughed a little. "Still, it was a stupid thing to do, Cameron. It didn't sound like Blackmore Inc. was going to pass on all the details to my firm, but either way, I never want to face that board again."

Cameron froze. "Will your firm ask questions?"

"Probably. And I'm not going to lie."

The waitress returned with their coffees, and Cameron took a scalding drink. When he looked up, Jackson was staring at him, her eyes filled with disbelief.

"Sorry," she mumbled, finding her cup. "It's just... well, I really didn't expect you to be here."

Cameron sighed. "Me neither, to tell you the truth. After I saw the paper, I spent the day all worked up. I was trying to find a way to manage the situation from Sydney."

"What did you come up with?"

"Nothing good. I had an assistant gather all the press you arranged, and I sent a letter to your firm praising you in detail."

Jackson's eyes widened. "Oh?"

"Not that kind of detail." He chuckled.

She blushed.

Should he tell her about the other things he'd done? Cameron shifted in his chair. Was she going to appreciate the gesture, or would she think it was excessive and invasive? Heat stole up his neck and onto his cheeks. He was blushing now, too, for God's sake.

He cleared his throat. "I...um...well, I also paid your rent for a year."

Jackson froze. "What?"

This wasn't going well. He had to just get it all out.

Cameron drew in a breath. "I know it's a little strange, but I was worried you'd lose your job. Because of me. And I knew I wasn't going to lose my job even though I had an affair at work, the same as you." He glanced over at the deep lines in her forehead. "Look, it just didn't seem right. And you mentioned how expensive your apartment was now that you'd moved out from your ex's place. And your ten-year plan..." Cameron scrubbed a hand over his face. "This isn't sounding good, is it?"

Jackson rubbed her temples. And then she started to laugh. Just a little at first, but her smile grew. She shook her head slowly. "What the hell am I supposed to say to that?"

"Thank you?"

Jackson rolled her eyes. "You are an arrogant man, Cameron Blackmore."

He chuckled. "I've got a lot worse faults than that."

Cameron leaned forward and slipped his hand under the table, resting it on her leg. She didn't move away.

"Anyway, I did a couple of other things that we can talk about later, but nothing I was doing felt right." He slowly rubbed her thigh with his thumb. "Jackson, I didn't just come to the board meeting because I wanted to help you out. I came because I wanted to be there for you. Do you see the difference?"

She tilted her head a bit, regarding him warily. No.

He was going to mess this up if he didn't hurry. He just had to say it.

Cameron leaned closer. "I'm falling in love, Jackson. With you. That's what got me on that plane. So I could be with you."

She drew in a quick breath. Then, she reached over and rested her hand on his cheek. Leaning forward, she pressed her mouth to his. Dear God, that felt good. Her lips were so soft and warm, and she tasted like coffee and mint and something so right. He tilted his head for a better angle, but she was already a step ahead of him. Jackson opened her lips and tasted. And just like that, the kiss spiraled out of control. A hot, aching release of all the tension from the last few days. Her hands were in his hair and he was searching higher on her thighs.

The waitress loudly cleared her throat.

Right. They were in a public place. He released Jackson, letting his fingers linger on the soft skin of her neck, and she sighed.

"I've wanted to do that since you walked into the conference room today," she said with a small smile. She shook herself a little, and the smile disappeared. "But I still don't understand how this could ever work between us."

He had gotten through the last twenty-four hours without a heart attack, and that included a plane ride from hell. If he could make it through that, he could tell her this last bit.

"Well, I also took some time off," he said carefully.

"Right." She feigned shock. "So, Cameron Blackmore took a vacation from work?"

"Yep. And I left Derek in charge."

Jackson paused. "For how long?"

"A couple months," he said softly. "I was hoping I could spend it with you."

"In that apartment you just paid for?" Her eyes danced with laughter.

"If you want. Or we could go somewhere you've always wanted to go." He pointed to her purse. "You have that little red book with you?"

She nodded and pulled it out. He took it out of her hand and opened to the first page, filled with school-age script. "Why not Paris?"

She frowned. "But on a plane?"

"I have a whole bottle of pills for that," he said. "You're also welcome to try more traditional relaxation techniques with me. First class has a little private space." He raised his eyebrows at her, and she smiled a little.

Cameron took a deep breath. "Seriously, it'll be tough, and I may need a break before I board a plane again. But if we're going to have a shot at being together, I have to deal with my shit. It might take a while, but I'll find a way."

Jackson found his hand and laced her fingers with his. "So you're moving in?"

"If you want me," he whispered.

The corners of her mouth turned up. "You already

know I do." She closed her eyes, and when she opened them, she smiled. "You're still here, right in front of me. I can't get over it."

"Does this mean you're open to revising your ten-year plan?"

Her eyes met his directly. "Yes, but I'm starting to suspect the old adage is true—the best laid plans often go awry."

"Maybe," he said, squeezing her hand. "But this is the best version of *awry* that I can think of."

* * * * *

COMING SOON!

We really hope you enjoyed reading this book. If you're looking for more romance, be sure to head to the shops when new books are available on

Thursday
26th July

LET'S TALK
Romance

For exclusive extracts, competitions
and special offers, find us online:

f facebook.com/millsandboon

@millsandboonuk

@millsandboon

Or get in touch on 0844 844 1351*

For all the latest titles coming soon, visit
millsandboon.co.uk/nextmonth